FILTHY BOSS

FORBIDDEN SERIES

BIANCA COLE

Filthy Boss Copyright © 2022 Bianca Cole

All Rights Reserved.
No part of this publication may be reproduced, stored, or transmitted in any form or by any means, electronic, mechanical, photocopying, recording, scanning, or otherwise without written permission from the publisher. It is illegal to copy this book, post it to a website, or distribute it by any other means without permission.

This novel is entirely a work of fiction. The names, characters and incidents portrayed in it are the work of the author's imagination. Any resemblance to actual persons, living or dead, events or localities is entirely coincidental.

Warning: the unauthorized reproduction or distribution of this copyrighted work is illegal. Criminal copyright infringement, including infringement without monetary gain, is investigated by the FBI and is punishable by up to 5 years in prison and a fine of $250,000.

Book Cover Design by Deliciously Dark Designs

CONTENTS

Blurb		v
1. Tessa		1
2. Tessa		9
3. Bryson		21
4. Tessa		33
5. Bryson		43
6. Tessa		50
7. Bryson		57
8. Tessa		70
9. Bryson		78
10. Tessa		84
11. Bryson		93
12. Tessa		103
13. Tessa		112
14. Bryson		119
15. Tessa		126
16. Bryson		132
17. Tessa		142
18. Bryson		148
19. Tessa		157
20. Bryson		165
21. Tessa		173
22. Tessa		180
23. Tessa		187
24. Bryson		198
Epilogue		206

Also by Bianca Cole 219
About the Author 221

BLURB

FILTHY BOSS

I broke the number one rule within hours of accepting my position as acting CEO.

I kissed my employee, but I didn't know she was my employee.

The next day, she walks into my office.

She has stumbled on evidence of embezzlement going on under my nose.

It's my first day on the job, and it's not going well.

I panic, telling her to mind her own business.

So she quits.

As much as I don't want to admit it, I need her help.

It means I've got to do something I never do—beg her to come back.

The problem is, anytime we're in the same room, I can't focus on anything but making her mine.

And if feelings get involved?

Yeah right. I'm Bryson Stafford and I don't let feelings get involved.

But Tessa has shown she's the exception to every rule.

1

TESSA

It's Friday evening, and I'm driving home early from work. Mrs. Davis gave me two hours off this afternoon to get away early for my trip to celebrate my recent engagement. As I'm driving down the highway, my attention lands on the ring on my finger.

I can't believe we're engaged. It all feels like a dream still. Initially, I felt a little anxious as it was such a grown-up step, but it became more exciting as the week wore on.

The chiming of a text notification breaks my train of thought, but I don't consider looking at it. Ever since my brother's death two years ago, I've been extra careful while driving, even though it was a freak accident.

I let out a shaky breath. It has been two years since Jack died in the head-on collision with a lorry and two years since Ted and I got together. I could never have imagined back then I'd be engaged to Ted, my brother's best friend.

The text is probably from him checking in with me—I want to surprise him by arriving home early. He's taking me on a mini-break to celebrate. Where we're going is a surprise. I should be over the moon Ted's arranging something for me, but I'm not too fond of surprises. I'm used to being in control.

I pull up in the driveway of our quaint little house, reaching over to retrieve my phone and unlock the screen to see the notification is from Kirsten, Ted's friend and colleague. I open the message and gasp.

It's a nude picture of her, which she sent to the wrong person. I delete the image and stow my phone away in my bag, getting out of the car. Our house is on the outskirts of Wynton in a nice little cul-de-sac. The rent is expensive, but Ted insists we need to live somewhere nice.

I head inside, shutting the door and walking into the hallway, setting my bag down by the door.

"Fuck me, Teddy Bear," a woman's voice echoes through the house, and I freeze.

I know that voice—It's Kirsten. Ted's colleague and the woman who sent me a naked photo on my way home. The noises echoing through the house toward the hallway are sickening.

"Fuck, yeah, baby. You feel so damn good," Ted grunts.

Kirsten's moans and Ted's animalistic grunts fill the air. I remain paralyzed in the hallway. My mind is a blank mess, and I've got no idea what to do. I don't need to see what is happening, but I can't stand here and wait for them to finish.

My heart aches as I listen to my fiancé fucking another woman. I can't believe Ted would do this to me. Why did he even bother asking me to marry him last week?

I'm heartbroken. Ted has betrayed me and is balls deep in his colleague. Did we rush into this relationship too quickly after I lost my brother?

For a while now, I've doubted whether he truly loves me the way I love him. Then he turned it all around and proposed to me last week, making me believe he did. It feels like he has ripped my heart from my chest.

How can I even face him?

I force my trembling legs forward. The image of them at it like rabbits on my kitchen island imprints in my mind and something snaps inside me.

I prepare my God damn lunch on that island. I bet this isn't the first time they've fucked here. A shiver runs down my spine as I consider all the places in *my* house they may have. "What the hell are you doing?" I say, my voice trembling.

Kirsten yelps as Ted stops thrusting into her and jumps away from the woman he'd been inside. His face turns ghost white as he glances between Kirsten and me.

Kirsten sits on the kitchen island, smirking at me. There's not an ounce of regret on her face at being caught, and I wonder if she'd sent me the photo on purpose.

It makes me sick that I've had her over for dinner countless times. I almost considered her a friend, but no friend would fuck another woman's fiancé. I can barely work out whether I'm hurt or pissed right now.

Ted steps toward me. "Baby, it's not what it looks like. I—"

I hold my hand up. "Don't even bother, Ted. Get out of here now." I glare at him. Then I turn to face Kirsten. "Both of you."

Kirsten's lips shift into a tight line. "Are you kicking us out?"

"Yes, get the fuck out of my house. I pay most of the rent for this place." I glare at Ted, and he starts pulling his clothes on, dressing. He doesn't seem to intend to fight for this or me, and that hurts.

Kirsten hasn't moved. I turn my attention to her and cross my arms over my chest. "I'm waiting for you to get dressed and get out of my house."

"Fine." She moves and pulls her dress over her head. "You can be a real uptight bitch, Tessa. We thought you might be into this, sharing."

That is the last straw.

Is she joking?

What the hell did she think I'd be into? Another

woman fucking my fiancé. I grab a vase off the side and throw it at her. She ducks, and it smashes against the wall.

Her eyes go wide, and she runs for the door. "Fucking Psycho," she shouts, twisting the knife as she grabs Ted's hand, and he allows her to pull him out of the house.

Good riddance.

As the door slams shut, I stare at the wall of the empty kitchen for so long. I'm not sure my mind has processed what just happened. I'm alone in my huge overpriced house, and everything hits me like a ton of bricks. They have turned my entire world upside down. I need a drink, but because Ted is teetotal, we have no alcohol in the house.

Before I know it, I'm in my car. As I pull onto the freeway and drive back into Wynton, I'm not even sure where I'm going or what I'm doing. I come upon the welcoming neon lights of a little hole in the wall dive bar. A place where no one will know me, and I don't have to worry about looking like a fool. A place I wouldn't be in danger of embarrassing myself in front of colleagues.

I walk into the bar and head straight for a free stool. A friendly face is beaming at me. Initially, she is a taunt with her fit, petite frame and bright blonde hair—similar to Kirsten.

As the night wears on, I get to know more about Elena, the bartender. She works shifts at the bar to pay her way through Hendall University and get a degree in sports medicine. Her goal is to train an Olympic team after getting out of college.

She lives on her own and is vocal about how she is doing fine without a man in her life, without me even mentioning the subject. I desire to be as strong, independent, and in control of my destiny as this woman seems to be.

Elena listens to me rattle on about Ted cheating. She is so understanding for a woman I've just met. She makes me feel like everything will be okay, or perhaps that's the alcohol.

By the end of the night, I'm drunk. Many of the older bikers offer to take me off Elena's hands. She tells them no way in hell.

I can't remember much else of the night. The rest is a blur as I leave the bar while Elena closes up.

She tells me to wait up because I'm in no condition to drive. I have no choice when I realize she has taken my car keys.

I WAKE the next morning to an awful hangover and the realization that I can't afford to live in my house any longer since Ted helped pay the bills. There's no use in me struggling through trying to pay for such a huge place for myself.

Elena enters, carrying a takeout bag and a box of aspirin. "Hey, Tessa, how are you feeling?"

Her voice is far too loud, and I grip my aching head. "Not great," I grumble.

"Here, take these." She hands me the aspirin and a bottle of water. I do as she says, taking the aspirin.

"Thank you. You didn't have to—"

"Nonsense, you had an awful evening last night. I'm happy to help out."

I force a smile at her before taking the aspirin and settling back down on the sofa.

She rummages through the takeout bag and pulls out a burger and fries, passing them to me. "You need to eat. It will help with the hangover."

My stomach rumbles as the smell of greasy fries fill my nostrils. "That's kind of you."

She sits down next to me and pulls out her burger and fries. We sit in comfortable silence, eating our burgers and fries. Once we're both finished, she turns to face me. "Did you think any more about my proposal last night?"

I try to rack my brain over what proposal she's talking about. My brow furrows. "What proposal?"

"Wow, you were drunker than I thought." She laughs. "You said you need to find a new place to live because your house is too expensive. I said I've got a spare room here and would welcome a roommate who can split the rent and bills with me."

I can't remember mentioning I need to find a new place. After talking it over, it doesn't sound like such a terrible idea.

The house Ted and I are renting is too expensive even

for both of us. At least this way, I can save some money. Ted and I had been living beyond our means.

I agree, feeling surprised I've got a new place to live within the space of twenty-four hours, and hopefully, a new friend.

2

TESSA

Three months later...

The blaring alarm wakes me from a terrible dream. I release my arm from under my duvet cover, searching for it. Finally, I grab the device, pulling it under the covers with me and hitting the snooze button.

I lay there with my hand against my forehead for a moment, staring at the ceiling fan. Despite loving my job, it's a struggle to get out of bed early. I've *never* been a morning person.

I force my legs out first, placing them on the floor. The cold from the wood spreads through the bottoms of my feet and my legs, sending a shiver up my spine.

It's only six in the morning, and I don't have to be in until eight, but I need the time to get ready. This is the time to get my head on straight and have my full quota of caffeine before facing the inevitable stampede on the streets outside.

I stand, stretching my arms above my head, before heading into the compact kitchen of our little apartment. Two months ago, I moved in with my friend, Elena. I'd been so used to living in a suburban area of Wynton. In a three-bedroom house with a spacious kitchen and all the amenities with Ted.

It's been three months since our breakup, and there's no denying it still stings. Elena likes to tell me constantly that he isn't worth it. I've been avoiding going to the bar she works at lately since she lectures me about moving on, attempting to push me toward one of the patrons.

She is *right*. Ted isn't worth it, and he never was. In a sense, he saved me from making a *huge* mistake, but it's not so easy to move on when you lose your fiancé and the future you expected all at once. We had plans to get married and have kids, and it's hard to let that go.

I pull down a mug from the cabinet above the coffee maker.

The shouts and screams of Ted's colleague, Kirsten, still resonate through my mind even to this day. The image of them *forever* imprinted on my mind. It was like a double punch to the gut. Ted had proposed to me only a week before, and like an idiot, I'd said yes.

I haven't seen him since, even though he begs for me to meet him so he can explain regularly. There was no chance in *hell* I was letting him explain anything. It was simple. He fucked another woman, end of story.

I pour a mug of coffee and sit at the island, slowly sipping it.

After I've drained every drop, I head for the bathroom, removing my sleep shirt and pajama shorts, throwing them into the small hamper in the corner.

I turn on the shower and get in, allowing the water to wash over me. I try not to think about Jack, my brother, but it's impossible. I can't shake the dream I'd had standing at his grave, the rain falling around us as we stood there, saying goodbye.

Once I've finished, I wrap my towel around me and walk back into my bedroom. I stare at the wall, lost in thought as I dry my hair.

"Hey, aren't you going to be late for work?" Elena pops her head through the door to my room.

I glance at her and then at the clock on the wall.

Shit.

I have been so distracted in my head that I've wasted time. "I'll be leaving in a minute. Why are you up so early?"

She shrugs and then bounds into my room, flopping down onto my bed. "I couldn't sleep." She cocks her head to the side. "You were thinking about him again, weren't you?"

I sigh heavily. "It's hard not to. I had a bad dream about my brother, and it dredged everything back up."

Her eyes soften. "I'm sorry. We'll do something fun tonight to get your mind off things. Come by the bar." She beams at me.

I nod, despite not feeling in the mood to do anything. I move to my wardrobe and pull out a gray double-breasted blazer, pulling it on over my white blouse.

I turn to Elena. "How do I look?"

Elena smiles. "Like a million bucks."

I laugh. If it weren't for Elena, I'm not sure what state of mind I'd be in right now. "Thanks, I best get going. I'll see you later."

She stands and pulls me into a tight hug. "Don't let anything get you down. You're a strong, independent woman."

"Thanks, Elena." I can't help but smile. "What would I do without you?"

She shakes her head. "I honestly don't know."

I grab my shoulder bag and head out into the busy street. I'm never late and don't intend to start now. I interned at the Stafford Financial Group during my last year at Hendall University. They were impressed with my abilities as an analyst and hired me full-time. Within six months of working there, I was promoted to an accounting analyst with my own office.

Anytime I feel my confidence slipping, I remind myself of my achievements. I don't need a man like Ted in my life. All I need is myself. I'm pretty sure Elena's rubbing off on me.

I make my way across the busy street and into the tube station. Hundreds of people rush down the stairs, surrounding me. I've made it with one minute to spare as the train rushes toward the platform, and everyone pushes onto it. I look over the sea of swaying faces on the subway as the smell of body odor and greasy breakfast fills the air, making me wrinkle my nose.

I reach the end of the line and scramble to get off the train, heading up the steps, despite the crowd budging me. Everyone is in a hurry to get to work on time. I head back onto the ground level. The towering structures of glass and steel rise, blocking the nearly *full* morning sun.

My building is opposite the station, and I'm glad when I make it across another busy street and head through the revolving glass doors. I breathe a sigh of relief at the sight of the gleaming, freshly polished marble and the sterile chic interior. It's a calming sight—logical and angular.

I march up to the front desk passing the security guard. "Good Morning, Marlon." I greet him with a quick smile.

"Morning, Tessa, have a great day." He smiles.

"You too."

"Good Morning, Anna," I say to the receptionist, who's typing frantically at her computer.

"Oh, hey, Tessa, nice day," she says absentmindedly and returns her attention to her screen.

I sign myself in and scan my badge before heading for the elevator. There's a group of people queued and waiting to go up, and I pile in with the rest of my colleagues.

All of us stand perfectly erect like foot soldiers awaiting deployment orders. This part of the morning always makes me worry about how bad my posture is, so I adjust the straightness of my back to fit in.

The doors open, and I struggle to get to the front and get out, walking down the corridor toward my little office at the back of the accounting floor.

I share a few cordial smiles and good morning greetings with my colleagues in passing. The door to my office is a welcome sight. I let myself in and shut the door behind me, sitting behind my desk and letting out a *long*, shaky breath.

My heart breaks a little as I glance down at the photo on top of my desk. My mom had a picture of our last family trip framed before my brother's accident. I stare at it a moment, lost in the heartache of how much I miss him.

Finally, I move my attention to the stack of ledgers on my desk, letting out a *sharp* exhale. I run my fingers through my hair, reaching into the left-hand pocket of my blazer. I pull out my reading glasses, putting them on. The silver pen that sits aligned with the writing guard under the mound of ledgers is in my hand within seconds.

I smile to myself and scan the room, and I take comfort in being in my second home before diving into the work and losing myself in numbers.

My hands fly across the keyboard as I work through one file at a time. If I weren't so preoccupied, I probably would have congratulated myself on how much I've done today. I'm too lost in the rhythm of work to register how well I'm getting on.

I stop for a moment and take a sip of the coffee I'd brought back from lunch. I'd only stopped ten minutes to grab a sandwich and a cup of coffee to bring back to my office. I don't have time for lunch. My new formula for getting work done is working until I'm too tired to keep going.

I intend to be the most productive analyst on the floor. I was promoted soon after joining, and I need to prove that I'm worth the *extra* pay and office. I'm here to win. Who needs breaks or sanity? Both of those things are pretty overrated.

I can hear my mom's lecture now.

Sweetheart, you know that's how people end having heart attacks before they're thirty years old and end up having to have organs replaced.

I take a long breath and glance at the outbox of my office. It's *stacked*. If I worked anywhere else, there would probably be someone around for me to high-five, but this isn't that *kind* of place.

I smile as I lose myself in numbers, as everything else fades into the background. I feel better than when I woke this morning as I scoot backward on my wheeled office chair to give myself room to open the drawer on my right and remove my leather shoulder bag.

I stand from my seat and turn off the desk lamp when a *ding* from my email rings out. I'd forgotten to turn off my desktop. I sit back down in my chair, the work bug pulling me back to my computer.

What could it hurt to take a look?

I put my glasses back on and slide closer to the screen, opening a file I've been sent. There are several expense sheets attached, which I open one by one. I pull out my pen and calculator to process the numbers. Everything is going well, as it's your run-of-the-mill expense reports for The Go-To Construction company doing some outsourcing for the general hospital. Until, suddenly, I hit a *snag*. Probably because I'm tired, and my brain isn't functioning right.

I shake my head and start the calculations over again. Then, run them through the accounting software on my computer to be certain. I'm stumped when everything comes out the same.

How is this possible?

There shouldn't be this many discrepancies, especially not from the Stafford Financial Group. It must be a mistake somewhere along the line. I need to get a second opinion, so I print off the sheets and grab them, heading toward the office of my department supervisor. Maybe, she can make some sense of this, and hopefully, she's still here as it is late.

My sensible flat shoes make slapping sounds as I walk across the tiled floor toward Mrs. Davis' office. I peer through the cracks in the blinds to find the lights are on. I rap on the door with my free knuckle.

"Come in," Mrs. Davis calls.

I open the door and pop my head in.

"Oh, Tessa, hello, dear," Mrs. Davis says.

She smiles at me from behind her reading glasses, which have slid down her nose. She reminds me of my old English teacher, with her gray hair piled on top of her head in a messy bun and her face patterned with deep wrinkles. She has always been a caring, mothering woman from the moment I arrived here, which puts me at ease to bring anything up with her that I feel out of place.

"Hi, Mrs. Davis. I wondered if I could ask you something. I know it's a bit late, and you're probably ready to go home, but could you take a look at this for me?" I hold the printed file up. "I'm stumped."

Mrs. Davis motions me inside. "No problem at all, honey, let me take a look."

I walk in and close the door behind me before placing the file in front of her. I open it to the appropriate section and point to the offending figures. "You see, here is where I'm having trouble. I received this in an email a little over half an hour ago, and I've been wracking my brain to decipher it, but it always comes out to that number."

"Hmm." Mrs. Davis pushes her glasses closer to her eyes as she lifts the file to get a better look. She hums a little under her breath as I watch her eyes move back and forth over the sheet, taking in *all the* numbers.

"If this is correct, I think I've stumbled upon something shady."

"What do you mean, dear?" Mrs. Davis looks at me over the thick rims of her glasses.

"Well, you see here where it talks about health and wellness accounts?" I touch the section on the page.

"Yes." Mrs. Davis's eyes follow my finger.

"If this is accurate, it means the money they say they transferred in the health and wellness accounts isn't being used for health care. They're not even allowing employees access to the money, and it is being funneled elsewhere. From the looks of it, it is to the tune of a quarter of a million dollars in the last six months. Which means—"

"Yes, I'm well aware of what that means," Mrs. Davis cuts me off abruptly.

As if she is afraid of something. I assume it's because if this were to be discovered, we'd have the feds breathing down our necks, which is the last thing any company wants.

After a long and thoughtful pause, Mrs. Davis removes her glasses altogether and chews on them. "Tessa, I need you to be completely honest with me."

"Yes, Mrs. Davis," I reply.

"Have you talked to anyone else about this?" Mrs. Davis turns to look at me.

"No one at all. You're the first person," I reply.

Mrs. Davis breathes a heavy sigh, slumping back in her chair. She takes another look at the file. "How did you come to have this?"

"What do you mean?"

"Well, it says this file is for the third floor. Why do you have it?" Mrs. Davis queried.

I shrug. "The only reason I opened it was because it showed up in my Inbox."

"Okay, well, I wouldn't worry about it, as this is something they'll deal with on the third floor. We're probably taking it out of context."

"I hope so," I add.

"As I said, I wouldn't worry anymore about it."

It's probably best I go home and forget about this, at least, until tomorrow. I turn to leave, bidding Mrs. Davis good night.

Mrs. Davis stops me. "Oh, and Tessa."

"Yes, Mrs. Davis?" I glance over my shoulder.

"Due to the fact this is a *fluke*, I wouldn't go around mentioning it to anyone else, alright? It'll only lead to gossip and a commotion. Our competition could take advantage of this information." She pauses a moment. "It would lead to the loss of your job, and we don't want that to happen, do we?"

My brow furrows at the threat in her voice.

"You've got a promising career ahead of you, and sometimes sacrifices need to be made to further said career. I'm sure you understand."

Rage floods me, heating my entire body. Something *shady* is going on, and Mrs. Davis wants me to brush it under the carpet. Not only does it go against my morals, but I can't overlook the truth of the numbers—no matter what.

I'll keep it to myself for *now*. The evidence needs to be taken above my supervisor's head, which means I need to take it to Bryson Stafford. I've hated the man ever since I started here, even though I've never met him in person.

Before I started, he did my telephone interview and was a complete and utter asshole. The problem is, I don't have the guts to take this to Abraham Stafford. He's *very* intimidating, and to be honest, I'm not sure he's been about much lately due to health issues.

"I understand perfectly," I say through gritted teeth. "Good night." I shut the door to her office.

I have a feeling I've made it past the honeymoon period of my job. Something tells me it's all about to take a turn for the worse. I'm about to unearth all the dirty secrets this corporation holds, and I'm not sure I'm ready to deal with it.

Especially if it requires me to make compromises and allowances for things that go against everything I stand for.

Is everything in life going to turn out like this?

First, my relationship with Ted and now my job. It feels like everything I touch turns to shit.

3

BRYSON

The sunlight dips below the towering buildings that rise across Wynton's skyline as I gaze out of the floor-to-ceiling windows of my office that line the entire wall.

I grab my jacket off the back of my office chair, shrugging it on and pressing the intercom on my phone to my secretary. "Anne, can you make sure Tom has the car ready for me, please?"

"Of course, sir, right away."

I tap my foot, waiting for her to tell me Tom's ready. I glance once more at the towering monuments of steel and glass surrounding me that penetrate the thick cover of clouds in the ever-darkening sky. They shimmer in the light of the moon, and street lights as distant sirens wail their ominous calls of death and destruction.

"Sir, he's ready for you."

I tear my eyes from the buildings and head for the

door. "Thanks, Anne. Don't work too late," I say, walking past her desk.

"Of course not, Bryson. See you tomorrow."

I give her a nod and head for the elevator. The door slides open, and I step inside, pressing the ground floor button. The lavish and grand entrance is empty as I step out of the elevator. It makes me swell with pride every time I walk through here. Our family's name is displayed in lettering above the entrance desk. It's ours, or more importantly, mine. I'm the eldest son set to inherit and become CEO.

The satisfying squeak of my leather loafers against the marble floor fills the air as I make my way to the revolving glass door and out into the fresh spring air. I stay back toward the doors waiting for Tom to arrive, as businessmen rush by yelling into their cell phones while other people laugh and chatter together. Mothers drag their screaming and laughing children down the street.

This is the worst part of the day. For a moment, with the hustle and bustle surrounding me and the smoggy claustrophobic atmosphere flooding the air. I can't wait to get off the street, even though I'm less than eager to attend the meeting with my father.

What is the meeting about?

It's likely my days as a carefree partying bachelor are over. My father has called me and my brother, Theo, to his house. There is only one reason he would call a meeting so suddenly. I'm certain that he will announce who will take over his role as CEO. If he goes with tradition and hands it to the eldest, it will mean I need to clean up my act.

It would be worth it, though. There's no way in hell I'm letting my father hand the company over to my little brother, Theo. Something tells me it won't be plain sailing. I've never exactly been my father's *favorite.* Theo is serious and driven about the business, whereas I spent a lot of time partying.

The screech of tires coming to a stop at the curb breaks my stream of thought.

My limo pulls up in front of me, and Tom jumps out. "Good evening, *sir.* Another long hard day at work?" Tom asks, opening the door for me.

"Yes, it's been tough." I run a hand through my hair and pass the heavy briefcase into Tom's outstretched hand. "I've had to lug around this briefcase and pretend like I was interested in spending five hours on this new deal for Mr. Gates. I'm meeting with him at eight in the morning tomorrow. So, I'll need an early pickup."

He nods. "Of course, sir. No problem."

I slide into the black leather seat of the limo as Tom slams the heavy door shut with a forceful thud.

He gets into the front, and the privacy screen comes down. "Am I right in thinking you're headed to your father's this evening, or do you need to swing by your home first?"

"Yeah, straight over to my father's house. Thank you, Tom." I respond, sighing and resting my head against the seat. I rub my tired eyelids with two fingers.

We pull away from the curb and join the herd of vehicles on the bustling evening roads. It promises to be a frustrating ride to my father's house on the other side of the city. And then, after the meeting, it will be an even worse ride home. Anxiety floods my gut as impatience to get this damn meeting over and done with grips me.

"Hey, Tom."

Tom glances in the rearview mirror at me. "Sir?"

"Would you mind taking a different route to the house? Go Broadway to South Street and then down. I think there'll be less traffic that way tonight. It might make it a little easier." I rub my forehead to relieve the pressure building behind my eyes.

"Yes, Mr. Bryson. I know the way well. Thanks for the tip." Tom replies, making a quick sharp U-turn and flipping the volume to Moby's "Natural Blues." It seems to play louder as the shiny black limo powers down the block.

I unbutton the top of my wrinkled Oxford shirt with one finger, feeling far too restricted and hot. I press my hands against the cool glass of the window to still the heat flooding my veins.

It doesn't help that my mind is a mess. Swap spreads, convexities, durations, and crack spreads explode in my head in a dancing chorus of confusion. They feel as if they trickle out of my sweaty fingers onto the glass of the window. This happens whenever I feel under pressure. I'm like a kid in college who has to cram everything in before a big test I need to ace the next day, or worse, in this case, considering I'll be at my father's house within half an hour.

I'm not as good at this financial stuff like my brother and never have been. It puts me at a disadvantage, but I know I can run a company, and that's all that matters. I need to make my father see I'm the right person to take over.

Theo is smart as hell, but he is quiet and reserved. He isn't self-assured like me. I would learn in time to get better with numbers or let Theo take care of the numbers while I took charge of the company's day-to-day running. A CEO doesn't have to worry about the day-to-day workings.

My father doesn't agree, as he has always been hell-bent on making sure that he is a leader rather than a boss. He's never satisfied with making everyone else do the grunt work and managing the business to ensure it runs smoothly. I'm sure I could make The Stafford Financial Group bigger and better than today, but he has to give me a chance.

My father must have done something right, though. Neither my family nor anyone at the company suffered major losses when the market crashed. Many other companies were much less fortunate. Companies had to downsize their staff, and some of them either had to outsource their labor to other countries or shut down altogether. As we drive along, I do my best to distract myself, watching people as we pass by.

It doesn't seem to take long to arrive at my father's

house. Perhaps it's because I'd been so caught up in my thoughts. We pass through the iron gate and up the long drive of my father's mansion, which opens to the grand frontage of the looming building.

As soon as the vehicle comes to a stop, I hesitate with my hand on the handle. I'm not sure why I'm *so* nervous. I'm *never* nervous. Tom makes it to the door to open it for me before I open it myself.

He smiles at me, holding my briefcase out for me to take.

I step out of the limo and take it. "Thanks, Tom."

"Is this good night, sir? Or would you like me to wait and give you a ride home?" Tom asks.

I consider his offer a moment and check my watch. It's late and unfair to ask him to wait for me. I could call a cab *pretty* easily, but I want Tom to be here when I get out, as he's someone I can trust to speak to after this dreaded meeting.

I clear my throat. "Tom, I'm sorry to ask this of you, but can you wait for me here, if that's okay? I know you've had a long day, but I'm not sure what I'm about to face in there." I nod toward the house. "I don't expect it to take long."

"No problem, Bryson. I'll wait right here for you."

"All right. I'll be out as quick as I can," I say.

"No rush, take your time." Tom climbs back into the driver's seat of the limo.

It's time to prove I can be calm under pressure as I stare up at the towering stone mansion in front of me. My father has changed homes so many times that the new house is so impossibly large, and the wrought iron doors feel more intimidating than ever before.

I need to get through this next hour. Then I can go home and chill. I hope everything goes as I expect, and I get the keys to the kingdom by the end. Deep down, I'm sure it won't be that easy.

I punch in the code and let myself into my father's home. He fitted a security system without the hassle of manual locks and keys.

Once inside the grand entryway, I walk towards the vast foyer, standing on a black and white tile floor. The expansive towering staircase juts out in front of me, wrapping around the circular hall. The house feels so *hollow*. Even more so today, as there are usually various members of staff walking around the house and one or two of Dad's ex-wives.

I contemplate how my father has lived his life. He has had more wives than I can count since our mother's death. They never make him happy, and they're all in it for the money, as my father is in his seventies now, and his most recent wife is younger than me.

I walk up the stairs, trying not to worry about the meeting. I have a feeling my dad isn't about to hand over the role of CEO to me, not after all the shit I've pulled in the past.

This late-night meeting makes it more likely. A way to keep me from making some kind of scene during the day.

Not that I'd make a scene, but it's the sort of thing he would do in case.

"Look who finally turned up," Theo says, smirking at me.

"I was busy. There were a lot of details of the deal for Mr. Gates I had to iron out today," I reply.

"Translation, there are a lot of things you're unfamiliar with because you spent too much time on fast cars and fast women rather than learning the business." He raises an eyebrow. "You should have finalized the Gates deal weeks ago." He walks ahead of me. "I told you you would regret not studying more when the time came." Theo leads the way down the long corridor to our father's room. "But if my hunch is right." He glances at me as he grabs the doorknob. "You may not have to worry about it, and you'll be able to go back to your life of philandering."

I open my mouth to defend myself, but before I have the chance, Theo flings the door open. He glides in, and I watch him cross the floor toward our father. I make my way in as well and close the door behind me. When I turn around, Dad has stood from his high-backed leather chair.

Even as an aging man with a bone disease, my dad is still intimidating. The harsh lines carved into his face, his large, deep-set eyes, and his gray hair give him a look that tells you he won't take any *shit*.

He opens his arms wide to pull me into a hug. My

father has always been a loving person for such a serious man, although most wouldn't believe it if they met him.

It contrasts the severe demands he puts on both of us. He has high standards for us in all aspects of life, standards I'm certain I'm yet to achieve in his eyes.

"Here, come take a seat." Dad gestures to the other two chairs. Theo rushes past me and sits down in the chair closest to our father. We sit in awkward silence for a moment.

"I know you both know why I've called this meeting. I apologize for the hour, but it is the best time. Old age," he sighs and points at both of us. "Avoid it if possible."

Theo chuckles, but the nerves dancing in my gut make it impossible to laugh. He looks between us once more, his gaze lingering on me longer than I'm comfortable with.

"Neither of you need to be uncomfortable. This is a family chat." He claps his hands together. "I'm proud of the men you've become. You've both been through rough spots we've had to iron out." Dad's eyes linger on me. "But, all of that's in the past, and we must concentrate on the future. I expect both of you to remember and respect your heritage as you carry out the tasks I'm about to set you."

"And what would those be?" Theo asks.

"Patience, I'm getting to that." He holds a hand out in front of him. "My health isn't what it used to be—"

"Of course." Theo rubs his forehead. "What did your

oncologist say when you went for your appointment today?"

"That's part of what I'm trying to get to if you would stop interrupting me." He shoots Theo a stern look.

"What appointment with the oncologist?" I sit up, ready to rush to my father's side.

Is he that ill?

Theo cocks his head. "If you bothered to visit more often, you'd know how unwell Dad has been."

Dad raises his hand. "I appreciate your concern, Theo, but there's no need for all of that. Your brother does what he can."

Guilt coils through my gut, as it's fine him saying it's not a big deal, but Theo's right, I haven't been here. I don't even know how ill my father is.

"So, what did they say?" I ask, my voice cracking in anticipation.

He takes a sip of his whiskey. "I spoke with the doctor today." He pauses. "They told me I have a little more than a year. The prostate cancer they thought they'd caught early enough turned out to be more aggressive than expected." Dad gazes at us calmly again before continuing, "It has spread to my bladder, and it will only be a matter of time before it spreads *further*. They can't operate." He shuffles slightly in his chair. "Do you understand why it's important to discuss the future of the company?"

"Yes, father," Theo says.

I can't speak, as my throat has closed up, and tears

prickle my eyes. It feels like someone has knocked the wind out of me. A clinching pain in my chest makes it difficult to breathe. My father is dying, and I've been off gallivanting about like an idiot at parties.

"Now that we've gotten the bad news out of the way, down to business. I have a plan I know you may not like." His eyes settle on me for a few beats too long. "I feel it necessary to see which of you is most capable of taking on the company after I'm gone."

I look up from my hands into my father's eyes.

"With that in mind. I've made provisions for both of you to take over my position as acting CEO of Stafford Financial Group for trial periods. Bryson, I will have you be the first to take over for three months, and we'll see how you do."

He turns his attention to Theo, who's smiling. "After, I will allow your brother to run the company as he pleases for the following three months. After six months, we'll have another meeting to determine who takes over the company."

"That sounds like a fair plan." Theo turns to face me. "What do you think, Bryson? Does it sound fair to you?" His gaze lingers on me, and I have got a sneaking suspicion he already knew about Dad's proposal.

It feels like all the air has been knocked out of me for a different reason. The news that my father won't hand the company to me doesn't shock me, not after the shit I've pulled over the years, but it doesn't hurt any less. I know I've got what it takes to run the company, but my father doesn't.

"It sounds fair, as long as you're up to the challenge," I say.

"I think the challenge is on you, not me," Theo says.

Dad stands from his chair, signifying that he is tired and ready for us to leave. "All right, boys, save the competition for the next six months."

We both stand and straighten our suits before hugging our father.

Theo shoots me a dirty look before he leaves the room.

My father's hands settle on my shoulders, forcing my attention to him. We gaze at each other for a moment before he says, "I'm counting on you, son."

I smile. "Don't worry, father. I won't disappoint you." I mean it this *time.*

4

TESSA

"Ray's bar, please, it's on Queen's street," I say as I slide into the back of the cab.

The taxi driver nods. "No problem, I know the place."

I let out a long sigh, relaxing into the seat. The taxi driver is friendly enough, and I engage in some small talk, hoping it'll distract me from the issue whirring around in my head.

As I politely listen to him talk about his kids and aging mother he struggles to care for on a pitiful salary, I realize it's not going to help. *All* I can think about is that The Stafford Financial Group is a den of thieves. They're no different from the other financial companies, and I'm a part of it now.

I don't care about the cost. There is *no* way I'm letting them brush this under the carpet. I'm thankful to see the flashing neon sign of Ray's bar come into view as the cab pulls to a stop. I thank the driver and tip him to help with his mother's care.

He thanks me in his broken English and tells me to call the number on his cab and ask for him if I need anything else. I make a mental note even though I *rarely* use cabs as they cost too much. I march toward the bar in desperate need of a drink.

I make it to the single door entrance of the bar, where a large, burly biker opens it for me with a smile. I thank him as I nearly had to shimmy past him to get into the place.

I glance at the chalkboard sign with my best friend's *all* too familiar handwriting. "Seat yourselves." I laugh at how short, to the point, and not in the least bit polite the message is, which is a testament to Elena's abrasive personality.

"Hey, *Tessa*," Elena calls, grabbing my attention. It's difficult to see more than her waving hand from behind the group of men sitting at the bar, as she's a short-ass.

She would be sure to correct me and say she's fun-sized rather than challenged in the height department. I don't let her height fool me, though, as Elena is a force to be reckoned with, not someone I would want to get on the wrong side of.

I walk across the *sticky* floor and make it to the bar, settling down on a stool opposite Elena.

She glances up at me. "Hard day at work?" She

continues drafting a beer while staring at me. Elena is good at multitasking.

She passes the pint into the awaiting fingers before making her way over to me and slapping her palms down on the bar.

"You've got no idea," I say.

"Oh, no, let me get you a drink," Elena says, grabbing a bottle down from the top shelf and taking it to the blender, and adding a mix of things. She pours the drink and heads over to me, setting a watermelon Cosmo down.

Elena nods. "All right, spill."

I sigh, wondering where to start. "Something odd happened at work today." I tap my fingers on the bar counter. "I was getting ready to leave, and I got an email in my work hub. I hadn't realized it was meant for the third floor. Anyway, I decided to go over the file."

"Figures." She shakes her head. "It's so like you to do work that isn't meant for you."

I frown. "I told you I hadn't noticed until my manager pointed it out."

"Let me guess you got flack for it?"

I take a sip of my drink. "Well, yeah, but that isn't the problem."

"Hmm, okay, carry on." She waves her hand in the air.

I cock my head to the side. "In the file. I came across figures that didn't make *any* sense. The money is going into health and wellness, but the people it's delegated to aren't allowed to use it."

"*Oh,* go on," Elena says, nodding her head.

"From the looks of things, this has been going on for the last few months, and no one has caught on to it, until now. I don't see how, though, because it adds up to a quarter of a million dollars."

"Oh, shit, now that's illegal," she whispers, her hands on her hips. "How are the feds not involved?"

I shake my head. "No one has caught onto it, I guess." I take another sip of my drink. "I took it to my department supervisor and told her about it. She told me I didn't need to say or do anything about it."

"Why the hell not?" she asks.

"Well, she told me it could cause a panic that would get me fired."

"Oh, she did, did she?" Her eyes narrow. "Well, honey, it goes to show you can't trust middle management. You know, that bitch is in on *it.*"

It's hard to imagine Mrs. Davis being in on a shady scam. "Do you think so? I mean, she's been there practically forever."

"Don't be so innocent." She rests a hand against her forehead. "The fact she's been there *so* long makes it more likely. They think they can get away with shit like this and brush it under the carpet. I'll tell you what you do."

"What?" I lean toward her.

"You take the evidence and go to the *big* boss. You tell him what's going on, and he'll sort it out. That way, if anything does go down, you're not the one responsible for getting anyone fired or investigated. That's another thing.

If she's in on it, you're going to find a target on your back. They could frame you."

A wave of uneasiness washes over me as I realize she's right. I need to take the evidence to Bryson, as I originally thought.

"Now, enough about work." She grabs my hand.

If she intends to force some so-called 'fun' on me, I will sprint out of this bar. "Yeah, what did you have in mind?" I ask, less than enthusiastically.

"Don't give me that tone of voice. You haven't even heard my idea yet."

"Okay, what did you have in mind?" I repeat in a cheerful tone.

"That's better, now do you see that scrumptious morsel seated at the end of the bar?" Elena motions to a tall man in his forties. He's not bad-looking, but he doesn't interest me in the slightest.

I shake my head. "No, thanks."

"I told him I would talk to you for him when you came in," she says.

"Ugh, Elena, no," I reply, bringing her attention back to me.

"Why not? He's kind of cute, right?" Elena asks.

"He's okay. I guess if you're into older men," I say.

"When will you be ready? It's about time you got over that jerk, Ted," Elena says.

"I'm *over* him, and I don't need to get laid to prove it," I reply.

"Fair enough, I get worried about you sometimes, is

all," she says, squeezing my hand. "He's not the only *hot* guy in the room, though. Some guy in a suit came in a few minutes before you. He's sitting at the back on his own." She nods her head toward the back.

I glance back at the way she looks, and my heart skips a beat. Hot is an understatement if you ask me. The guy she's referring to looks like a male model, and he's *way* out of my league.

She raises an eyebrow. "Why don't you say hello?"

I shake my head. "No way, he's out of my league."

Her brow furrows. "Tessa, you're a beautiful woman. He'd be lucky if you approached him."

I glance back at him, and his eyes meet mine, making my heart race and my body heat.

"Go on, what have you got to lose?"

She's right. What do I have to lose? I give Elena a small nod. "Okay, I'll speak to him."

She *squeals* and then grabs my hand. "Okay, let me fix you two some drinks." She busies herself, getting me another cocktail and pouring him a bourbon.

I glance back at him to find his eyes fixed on me. I can't believe I'm about to approach a guy in a bar. What if he refuses to talk to me?

Elena sets the two drinks down. "Get him, tiger."

I roll my eyes and then grab the drinks, standing and heading toward him. My heart is beating *hard* against my rib cage with each step I take. The closer I get to him, the more attractive he is. Suddenly, my confidence is waning, and my whole body is trembling. I consider heading right past him and into the bathroom.

Then he speaks, "I hope you're coming over here to speak to me." He flashes me a heart-fluttering smile. His voice is a deep and confident baritone.

He noticed I was losing my resolve to approach him and took it into his own hands. I nod. "Yes, if you don't mind. I saw you were on your own and…"

He smiles. "Take a seat. What's your name?"

"Tessa." I slide into the booth, setting down his drink.

He smiles. "Thanks for the drink." He extends his hand toward me. "It's lovely to meet you, Tessa. I'm Bry." His large hand encases mine, sending a shot of need through me.

"Nice to meet you too." I smile.

This guy can't be interested in me, as he's far *too* attractive. He is the most attractive man I've ever seen with beautiful, piercing blue eyes. His dark hair is longer on the top and shorter on the sides, and he has the perfect amount of stubble over his jaw. My eyes roam his muscled chest framed in an expensive white shirt.

"What brings you to this bar tonight?" he asks.

"I come here a lot. My best friend and roommate is the bartender." I nod toward Elena, who is glancing over at us. "How about you?"

He takes a long sip of his drink before speaking, "Rough night, not something I want to talk about."

I nod and drum my fingers on the table. "What would you like to talk about?"

He laces his fingers together on the table. "*You.*"

Heat floods my entire body, making my pussy wet and my thighs clench. He stares at me with such a hungry, fierce look in his eyes, and his voice makes me melt.

"What do you do for work?" he asks.

"I'm an accounting analyst."

He licks his lips, drawing my eyes to them. "Hmm, sexy and smart."

The way he calls me sexy makes me heat more. My whole body is on fire right now. No one has *ever* called me sexy. "What about you?"

He shakes his head. "I told you. I want to talk about *you.*" His commanding tone sends a spark of need through me, making my pussy ache.

I can't believe how turned on I am as I stare into the oceanic eyes of this man. He asks me questions about my childhood and where I grew up. I answer him, reminiscing on my happy childhood, even though it dredges up some painful memories associated with Jack.

"Where is your brother now, then?" he asks.

I feel my throat close up. A pain clutches around my heart in my chest, and the blood *drains* from my face. This is the first hard question he has asked, and I'm not sure I can answer it. I glance up into those kind eyes. His presence *eases* a small ounce of pain. "H-He died two years ago." I swallow the lump in my throat.

Bry's eyes turn sad, and he takes my hand in his. "I'm so sorry… I didn't mean to…" He shakes his head.

I squeeze his hand. "Don't worry. You didn't know." I force a smile at him, even though it's hard to talk about Jack. I never talk about him anymore.

He sighs. "Where do you live?"

"Around the corner from here, why?"

"If you would like, I can walk you home." A smirk plays at his lips, and I know he expects me to *fuck* him. I'm not sure I'm *ready* to jump into bed with a man I just met. My body, however, is well and truly primed. I'm aching for him.

I shrug. "If you would like, but I'm not inviting you in."

His eyes seem to flash as if I've challenged him. "Okay, but I want to make sure you get home safe."

I nod. "Let me say goodnight to my friend and let her know I'm leaving." I turn and slide out of the booth.

Elena winks at me as I approach. "Looks like you two are getting rather *cozy* back there."

I smile at her. "Yeah, I guess. He's hot as hell." I glance back at him. "Bry offered to walk me home. I'll see you when you get back?"

She raises an eyebrow. "Surely, you'll both be busy when I get back."

I shake my head. "I'm not asking him in. I don't know him."

She sighs, resigned to the fact I'm not going to hook up with this guy. "All right, I'll see you at home then."

I turn around to find him standing right behind me.

He's so tall, as I gaze up into his sparkling blue eyes. "Ready?"

I swallow thickly, wondering if I'm going to be able to resist sleeping with this man. He's so hot I can feel a *pulse* ignite inside of me at the thought of his hands all over my body. This will be a true test of my willpower.

5

BRYSON

*C*hallenge accepted.

This stunning brunette thinks she won't invite me in, but I'll make sure she does. Her mind is telling her one thing, but I can see the way she's responding to me.

The pink flush in her cheeks spreads right down her neck and no doubt onto her *full* breasts. Her lips part in a way that makes me want to pull her to me and kiss her.

I came here tonight to drown my sorrows in as much bourbon as possible. To get my mind off of my father's plan and the fact he's dying. Instead, I'm walking this beautiful woman home.

The moment I set eyes on her, my cock was hard and ready, throbbing in my pants. I didn't even have to approach her. She approached me. She told me she's not inviting me in, and now she's reiterating the same thing to her friend. We'll see about that.

She spins around, and her eyes widen as she looks up at me.

"Ready?" I ask.

She nods her head, and I grab her hand. Her soft skin feels like *heaven* against mine. I want to feel every inch of her against me. My cock leaks precum into my tight boxer briefs as she bites her full bottom lip between her teeth. I *groan* at how turned on I am.

Tessa isn't my normal type. She's intelligent, naturally beautiful, and different from the girls I normally go for. It's been a while since I've been with anyone. The stress of work has been getting to me, and although I've been partying, I've been struggling to ignite *a desire* for any of the women I used to find attractive. It's been well over *eight* months since I last had sex.

Then Tessa walks into this bar, and I find myself as hard as nails. We step out together into the cool night air, and a shiver passes through her. Her hand clenching *mine tighter*.

I shrug my jacket off and wrap it around her. She grabs the jacket and pulls it more snuggly around her. "Thank you. Aren't you going to be cold?"

I shake my head. "No, I'm fine." I don't need to tell her I'm hot and bothered because she *lights* me on fire.

"How far is it to your place?" I give her a sideways glance.

"It's one block on the right."

I rub my hand over my jaw, wondering how I can *make* this walk last longer. I'm fairly confident I'll get this beauty to ask me in, but if she sticks to her guns, then I'll have to part from her *too* soon.

"How about we take a detour? I want to spend as much time with you as possible."

She flushes a pretty pink. "What kind of detour?"

I squeeze her hand gently. "You'll like it. Come on."

She searches my face for a moment before nodding.

"I love places filled with nature in the city." I lead her right toward the park nearby. It's dimly lit by the streetlights and the full moon above us in the sky.

Tessa looks up at me and smiles. "It's nothing like the countryside, though, is it?"

I shrug. "I wouldn't know. I've never been. I spend a lot of time in cities."

Her eyes widen. "Not even on vacation?"

I shake my head. "My vacations, even as a kid, were always in a city setting."

"Wow, you need to take a vacation in the countryside. It's far more relaxing."

I laugh. "Perhaps you can take me sometime?" I don't even know where that came from, as we've only just met.

Tessa tenses beside me, dragging her bottom lip between her teeth *again*. "Maybe."

I tighten my grip on her hand and jerk her to a stop, gazing into her beautiful emerald eyes. "Tessa, you're so beautiful."

She swallows hard, gazing at the floor. It's as if no man has *ever* called her beautiful.

"Has anyone ever told you that?"

She won't look at me, just gazes at the floor and shakes her head.

"It's a damn crime that they haven't. You should be told every day," I growl, finding myself oddly possessive of this woman.

I hook my finger under her chin and force her to look at me. There's no one around as we rest beneath an old oak tree in the park, only a few inches between us. She licks her lip, drawing my attention to them. My cock strains hard against the fabric of my pants, making me more desperate to kiss her.

I inch closer to her. "Tessa…"

Our lips meet in a tentative kiss, and I wrap my arms around her waist, pulling her tight to me. My tongue darts across the seam of her mouth, forcing it to open for me to plunder. A frantic need to *claim* her grips hold of me, and I find my hands snaking to cup her ass tightly, pulling her body close.

She gasps into my mouth as I grind my thick, hard cock into her lower abdomen, making her melt. Her arms wrap around my neck, and she pulls me tight against her. Her tongue tangles with mine as she comes *alive*, kissing me passionately.

My cock throbs against her, and my balls ache for release as she grinds herself against me. She wants this as much as I do. I let my fingers slowly trace up to her bare thigh, inching beneath her skirt. I groan as my fingers find her slick panties, soaking in her juices.

Tessa *moans* as I let my finger ease under the thin, wet

fabric, and I part her slick lips with my finger. I bite her lip gently and then trail kisses down her neck, pushing her back toward the tree. She gasps as her back hits the wood. "Bryson, we shouldn't—"

I silence her with a hard kiss, making her body relax into mine. Slowly, I allow my finger to ease into her slippery, tight pussy, groaning against her soft skin. She feels *perfect*. My cock is straining against the fabric of my pants, desperate to be inside of her.

She moans as I finger her pussy, lightly rubbing my thumb over her swollen, throbbing clit. Her eyes roll back in her head as I plunge *two* thick fingers inside of her. "Do you like that, baby?" I groan into her ear. "Do you like me fingering you right here in the park?"

She nods, biting her bottom lip. Her face is flushed, the prettiest shade of pink I've ever seen. *Fuck*. I want to fuck her right here against this tree.

I glance around, checking we're alone. The lights are dim, and no one would see what we're doing under this tree. I'm not used to being so crazy, but Tessa makes me insane. I drop to my knees and hike her skirt up to her hips, pulling her lacy panties down to her knees.

Tessa's knees tremble, and she gasps. "What are you—"

I clamp my lips down over her clit, and she *cries* out, bucking her hips toward me. I let my tongue circle her clit before dragging it right through her dripping wet lips. She tastes better than honey, so fucking sweet. I part them and taste her more deeply, grabbing my aching cock and rubbing it through the fabric simultaneously.

I *want* this woman more than anything.

She moans, lacing her fingers in my hair. I remove my mouth for a moment. "Do you like that, Tessa? Do you like me licking this naughty little cunt right here in the park?" I growl, rubbing my cock in my pants.

Her eyes widen at the word I use, but she bites her lips and nods.

"I want to hear you say it," I growl.

Her lips part deliciously. "I like it, Bryson," she gasps.

I return my tongue to her clit, and she jolts, writhing above me. Her whole body is wound tight as I ease my tongue inside her, tasting her sweet nectar again.

"Oh my God," she moans, lacing her fingers in my hair.

I shove *two* thick fingers deep inside of her and kiss and nip at her throbbing clit, making her moan even *louder.* Her whole body trembles in my hands as she gazes down at me lustily. I lick her clit and curl my fingers, finding the spot that makes her muscles flutter on the *edge* of the explosion.

"That's it, baby, come for me. I want to feel your tight little pussy come all over my fingers. I want to taste every drop of you as your cum floods from you," I groan, still gripping my straining length in my pants.

"Bry..." she moans my name as her orgasm breaks inside of her.

I pull my fingers from her slick entrance and lap up

every drop of sweet juice pouring from her. She bucks and writhes above me, eyes shut and mouth hanging open. She looks *so* fucking beautiful. Once I've licked every drop of her, I stand and kiss her hard, making her taste herself on my tongue.

She moans into my mouth, clawing at me for more. Her hips grind against the thick, throbbing length of me as she tries to get more.

"Fuck me," she gasps against my mouth. "Right here."

My cock gets so hard that it feels like it might rip through my pants. I smile at her, feeling triumphant that her resolve has well and truly shattered.

"You're a naughty girl, Tessa. You want my cock in that tight fucking pussy right here in this park?" I ask, glancing around to ensure we're still alone.

She bites her lip, moaning.

I unzip my pants and ease them down my hips, along with my boxers. My cock slaps against my shirt-clad stomach, and Tessa's eyes widen.

"I'm going to give you every thick inch, right here," I groan, fisting myself from root to tip.

6

TESSA

What the hell has gotten into me?

I *moan* so loud at the sight of his *huge* cock standing upright and ready — a bead of white, pearly precum glistening on his thick, swollen head. His fingers tease at the buttons of my blouse, and he unbuttons them, revealing my breasts clad in a lacy white bra.

He growls as he kisses my cleavage and then forces my bra down, revealing my hard, erect nipples. He takes one into his mouth and sucks, making it ache and harden more. Then it does the same with the other one. My pussy is dripping right now. My hand reaches for his thick cock, and I pump it with my fingers, feeling him throb against my palm.

I drop to my knees on *pure* instinct, desperate to taste his *huge* cock. No longer aware of where I am or what I'm doing, only the thick length of him pulsing in my hand.

His fingers wrap around my wrist. "What are you doing?" he *growls*.

I love it when he growls. He sounds half-beast, half-man. *Fuck*. I've never been this turned on in *all* my life. I'm always logical, but here with this man, I'm *wild* and untamed. "I want to taste you."

He *groans*, letting go of my wrist. I let my tongue lap up the thick, salty liquid beading on the tip of his straining cock, savoring the taste of him. I close my lips around the head, making him grunt and grab my hair.

My tongue swirls around his swollen crown, making more delicious precum leaks from his tip onto my tongue. I *moan* at the taste of him, humming as I slip my lips further down his *huge* length. I've never seen a cock this big, *ever*. It makes me even more wanton with the need to feel him deep inside of me.

I work my mouth further and further down his cock, trying to get my throat to take more of him each time. It makes me feel so needy for him to fill my aching pussy as he grunts and groans above me, tightening his fingers in my hair and pushing me deeper each time. I *moan* around his cock, tasting more and more of his salty seed as it spills into my mouth. I want him to cum right down my throat and swallow every drop.

I move all the way back up to the crown of his cock and let my tongue swirl the crown and then drag it down his throbbing, *hot* underside. His balls clench as I lick and tease them, making more thick precum spill down his shaft. I let my tongue drag up his long length slowly and make sure I get every last drop of the sweet, pearly liquid with my tongue.

His fingers tighten around my wrist, and he jerks me away from his cock, forcing me to my feet. "Your lips feel like fucking heaven," he growls, pushing me back against the tree stump. "But I'm ready to feel that tight pussy wrapped around my cock."

I never thought I'd like a man using *that* word during sex, but it gets me going like nothing *ever* has. Not to mention, I never thought I'd do anything like this in public, but it's thrilling. I'm too far gone to stop. I moan as he rubs the swollen crown of his cock between my slippery, wet lips, coating himself in my juices.

"Do you want to feel *every* inch of me stretching you?" he groans, capturing my bottom lip between his teeth.

I moan and nod.

"Tell me, Tessa," he growls.

"Yes, I want you to fuck me."

He groans and dips his fingers into my hips, lifting me and making me wrap my legs around his muscled waist. He uses the stump of the tree for support as he pushes forward and enters me hard and fast, making me *cry* out. His corded muscles rippling in his arms against the tight fabric of his shirt.

"Fuck," I moan, feeling inch after thick inch stretching me like I've *never* been stretched before.

His lips press against my neck, and he *groans* against me. "That's it, baby. Take my cock deep inside of you. You feel so fucking perfect and tight, Tessa."

I moan as he thrusts in and out of me, pinning me to the rough tree behind us. His fingers dig into my ass possessively, and he drives into me deeper and harder, going further than any man has *ever* gone. I claw at his back, pulling him closer to me. His lips close over mine, making me whimper.

I never thought I'd be this girl. Moaning and trembling as this man I don't even know fucks me outside in a park. It's more freeing and electrifying than anything I've ever known. I can feel him dragging me higher and higher as he claws one hand from my ass and rubs my clit, making me *cry* out.

Thank God, no one is around. It's late, and this park isn't often busy.

"That's it, baby, take every inch of my cock. *Fuck*. You feel amazing wrapped around me."

I moan louder, unable to think as he talks dirty to me. This man has already made me come by licking my pussy, but I can feel the pressure building and mounting inside of me. He's sending me right back to the edge of explosion with each hard, deep thrust of his throbbing cock. His balls slap against my ass as he fucks me harder.

He pulls out and sets me down on the floor. "Turn around, Tessa," he commands.

I do as he says, grabbing hold of the tree for support and arching my back. I stick my ass out for him, ready for more.

He groans and slaps my ass check, making me *gasp*. "Fuck, you're so perfect." He spreads my ass cheeks and runs a finger over my forbidden hole, sending a thrill through me. With one quick, hard thrust, he buries his *huge* length inside of me *again*.

I moan, rocking my hips backward to feel him thrusting in and out of me. He digs his fingers into my hips and holds me still. "I'm in control, baby."

I melt as he takes me against the tree, submitting total control to this *stranger*. He's like a man possessed as he drives into me again and again, reaching around to rub my clit. The way he makes me feel is unbelievable. The way he is fucking me is like a primal, animalistic mating. The pressure inside of me has me teetering on the edge of an orgasm.

He grunts and leans over my back, kissing my neck. "I want to feel you come all over my cock, baby. Come for me," he growls.

I *cry* out as my orgasm crashes through me, ten times more powerful than the first. I'm so hot as fire floods my belly and my limbs, making me tremble. I've never had an orgasm like it. My whole body convulses, and my pussy clamps down on his cock, making him *roar* as he explodes along with me.

I feel every thick, hot drop of his cum splash deep inside of me as he holds me tight. We're both breathing heavily as I remain resting against the tree, shaking like a leaf.

"Fuck," he grunts, pulling his thick cock from my wet pussy.

I stand up and hike my panties up, as they'd fallen

down to my ankles. His cum is dripping into my panties and making a mess of them as I straighten my skirt. I turn around to see him shoving his still semi-hard cock into his pants. He pulls me close and kisses me tenderly, making me melt for him again.

I can't quite believe I just did that. I didn't even use a condom, and I don't even know this guy. What the hell was I thinking? At least I'm on the pill still.

Bryson's lips part from mine, and he smiles at me. He drags my bra back up into place and then buttons my blouse, hiding my breasts from him and the world. He kisses me again, long and slow, making me moan into his mouth. I've just had *two* orgasms, and I want *more* from him.

"Come on, let's get you home." He grabs my hand and pulls me back toward the path.

We walk in silence, but it's not as awkward as I expect it to be. It's oddly comfortable. As if we didn't just fuck in public five minutes ago.

No man has ever made me feel the way he did. He is sexy as hell, and I *want* him *again*. Finally, we reach my apartment. "This is me." I nod at the front door and break the silence. "Thank you for walking me back and…" I feel the heat rushing through my body, heating my cheeks.

I still can't quite wrap my head around what we did.

His smile is so irresistible. "You're welcome, Tessa." He closes the gap between us, and his lips are on mine in a heartbeat.

I melt into his strong arms as they lock around me. A deep ache ignites with a desperate need to feel him inside of me again. His stubble grazes my soft skin, sending thrills through me. I want to fuck him again, so *badly*.

I deepen the kiss, allowing our tongues to tangle in a breathless and desperate kiss. His thick, hard cock presses into me, already ready. I can't invite him in, though. How the hell would I explain this to Elena?

I pull back, breathless, and *far* too aroused. I gaze up into the beautiful blue eyes of this man I've only just met and already fucked. "Well, thanks again," I say.

He captures my hand in his. "Wait, what's your number?"

I search his eyes for a moment, considering not answering, even though we just had sex. "Give me your phone."

He passes it into my hand, and I type my number in before passing it back to him. "There."

He smiles and kisses me again. "I'll text you later, baby."

I nod. "Good night, Bryson." I bolt up the stairs to my apartment and shut the door. It's as if I snap back to reality, and the true weight of what I just did hits me. I lean my back against the door and let out a long breath.

Holy shit, I fucked a total stranger in a park, and I *loved* it.

7

BRYSON

I'm doing my best to focus on the work in front of me, but my cock is as hard as a rock. Ever since last night, I'm like a *horny* teenager who can't control his urges.

Tessa is *all* I can think of. I texted her a few times last night, but she never replied. Then I tried ringing her this morning, and it went to voicemail. Maybe she regrets what we did. Usually, I don't want to see the women I fuck again, but Tessa is different.

The sex was unlike anything I've ever experienced—passionate and all-consuming. Tessa is *all* I want. She is *all* I can think about.

The first day as CEO and I can't concentrate at all. It is like this woman has derailed me entirely and thrown my life off track. If she doesn't answer my calls or texts, I'm going to that damn bar until she turns up. Her best friend works there. She admitted she goes there a lot, so that's where I'll be heading tonight.

My cock is throbbing in my pants even though I relieved myself half an hour ago in my private bathroom adjoining the office. It looks like I'll be wanking all day at this rate.

Tessa's face keeps flashing into my mind. She's not like the women that usually catch my attention. More often, they are blonde and caked in make-up. Tessa is a natural beauty with dark brown hair and bright emerald eyes. Her clothes were also far more conservative than women I'm generally with, but I get a feeling Tessa can make anything look sexy as hell.

My mind can't stop replaying our session in the park. The way she let me take her against the tree, it was so damn *sexy*. All I want to do is see her again, touch her again, fuck her again. Damn it. Tessa is mine.

I didn't believe anything could get my mind off the news my father broke to me last night. Then she walked into that bar.

I'd drunk more than I should have last night, so now I'm nursing a headache. Not to mention, after fucking that beauty, I couldn't sleep. I'd taken aspirin and drank about three cups of coffee this morning. It was all I could do to stay focused through the meeting with Mr. Gates earlier.

It is the first of many meetings I'll be expected to attend as acting CEO. The weight on my shoulders, increasing as the reality of the responsibility hits me.

Perhaps I should step aside and allow my brother to take over. Is being CEO worth it? It's all I've wanted for as long as I can remember—a chance to prove my worth. But, now, in this position of power, I feel the confidence in my abilities slipping. Am I up for this challenge?

I have to be for the sake of my relationship with my father.

I spent so much of my life doing things that brought shame to the family, especially as the media like to seize hold of any dirt they can get on us. The last opportunity to change my dad's opinion of me. I can't screw this up. I just can't. It's my only chance to make things right, to make my father proud of me before he's gone.

I stand and look out over the expansive city as I let out a long breath. Somewhere, Tessa is out there. I barely know her, but I *crave* her like a drug. Somehow, she has sunk her claws into me with her stunning smile and emerald green eyes—those eyes that I can't get out of my head. I scan the jutting buildings that glitter in the late morning sun.

They appear different to me now than they had the night before. I can't understand why. Perhaps because I learned my father is dying or because I met a woman who made me want to be different. Whatever it is, it's a strange sensation. For once, I feel less selfish and more vulnerable than ever before.

"Mr. Stafford?" A woman says from the doorway.

I turn on the balls of my feet. "Yes."

The woman is beautiful. The type of woman I'd

normally be drawn to *outside* the office, but as I drag my eyes up and down her tall, slender frame in a white pinstriped blouse and short skirt, I feel nothing—no attraction, no desire to fuck her.

What the hell has Tessa done to me? I never mingle business with pleasure anyway, as it would be unprofessional.

Her bright blonde hair is perfectly styled, framing her creamy complexion and heart-shaped face, but still, there's *no* excitement stirring.

She clears her throat. "I'm Charlotte. Your new secretary, sir."

I nod my head. "It's nice to meet you, Charlotte." She lingers by the door, and I narrow my eyes. "Is there anything else I can help with?"

"There is someone here who would like to speak with you," she says.

My brow furrows. "Does this person have an appointment?" I straighten my tie and jacket in anticipation.

"It's an accounting analyst from the first floor. She says there is an urgent matter that needs to discussing," Charlotte says.

"I see." I pinch my chin between my finger and thumb, wondering what the normal process is with employees demanding to talk to me. Surely, they should have an appointment?

"Should I send her in?" Charlotte motions to the outer office behind her.

"Yes, please," I say, watching as she opens the door a little wider. "Oh, and Charlotte…"

"Yes, Mr. Stafford."

I wince. "Please call me Bryson. I'm not my father." I perch on the edge of my desk, waiting.

"Of course, sir." She smiles before returning to get the woman from accounting.

The door opens, and my heart stops beating.

Tessa.

My mouth goes dry, my heart rate spikes, and my cock thickens and swells in my pants as the memories of fucking her last night hit me.

Tessa stares at me with her mouth ajar, looking as shocked as I feel.

Charlotte seems to notice the tension. "Is that all, sir?"

I tear my eyes from Tessa. "Yes, thank you."

She smiles before scurrying out of my office.

A silence settles between us as we stare at each other. My eyes rake over her curvy body, which I well and truly felt last night while I fucked her against that tree.

Her outfit is similar, as she wears a tight white blouse and a medium-length skirt. I notice her dark brown hair is no longer free and flowing around her shoulders, but tied in a bun, revealing her slender neck. A neck I *long* to kiss again. Those luscious, pink lips part as she closes her mouth. Her cheeks have turned red, and it makes me want to *take* her again even more.

Fuck.

My first night in charge, and I violated one of the number one rules as a CEO. I may have been unaware, but I know how bad this situation is. Perhaps she recognized me and thought she could exploit my position to get higher in the company. The thought hurts me more than it should.

Is that why she is here?

"I-I..." She shakes her head.

"What the fuck?" I ask, unable to think straight.

"Your... But..." She can't seem to get the words out.

I step toward her. "Didn't you recognize me last night, considering you work for my company?" I ask.

It seems a coincidence. If Tessa is about to insist on a pay rise, she can stuff it where the sun doesn't shine. I won't let her blackmail me.

She shrugs. "I'm a low-level accounting analyst. I've never had cause to meet you or see you around the office. I'm as shocked as you, sir." She can't meet my gaze.

I swallow hard. "Here, please take a seat," I say.

She steps forward and sinks into one of the plush leather chairs in front of my desk.

I'm trying to process what is going on right now. A few moments ago, I couldn't stop thinking about this woman. Now, here she is, sitting in my office, looking as stunning as ever. All I can think about is sinking every thick inch of my cock deep inside her tight pussy right here, bent over my desk.

I clear my throat. "After last night, we're more

acquainted than I *ever* am with my employees, Tessa." I can't keep the huskiness from my voice.

She flinches at my tone. "I can't believe I didn't put two and two together. Bryson, I knew the name, but…" She shakes her head. "I never thought you would be in a place like that…"

I shrug and eye her. "No reason for it to affect our professionalism."

She bites her full bottom lip. "I guess not."

"Why are you here, Tessa?" I ask.

"Well, sir."

Sir.

Everyone here calls me sir, literally, everyone. So, why does my cock jump in my pants at hearing it from her lips? She pulls out a folder from under her arm and opens it. "I received an email to my work hub last night for the third floor and—"

"Oh, I'm sure it happens all the time. You don't have to do other people's work. I'll alert them to their mistake."

Tessa shakes her head. Her cheeks are reddening, and her eyes fill with irritation. "I wish it were that simple, Mr. Stafford."

I *cringe* at her calling me by my father's name. "What else seems to be the issue, Tessa?"

"As I was going over the figures last night, I found a problem with the contract with The Go-To Construction company account. They've set up a health and wellness account for the contractors and their security, but the employees have made no withdrawals for the use of their health and wellness. All withdrawals have reverted to the company to the amount of a quarter of a million dollars," she explains, moving to my side of the desk to give me a better view. The way her hips sway as she walks makes me want to grab them and park her ass on my lap.

This is bad.

The problem with her getting this close is she's going to give me a better view of her tight body and the cleavage peaking over her unbuttoned blouse. All I can think of is how good her breasts looked, spilling over the top of her bra as I fucked her hard against that tree.

I can't focus on anything with her here. Not to mention, she's about to see what she is doing to me.

I slide my chair forward before she makes it over to me to hide my *bulge* in my pants. I look down for a moment at the spreadsheet and pretend to check over the figures.

As if I'm paying any attention to them. Any blood in my body has shot right into my throbbing cock. I'm not in a position to see straight, let alone think straight. The sweet jasmine scent of her floods my nostrils and fuels my lust.

"So, what do you think, sir?"

That word again. On her lips, it sounds so *filthy*. Most likely because all I can think about is fucking her again, right here in my office, bending her over the desk, while she screams it.

Damn.

I'll tell you what I think, Tessa. I think you should sit on my lap while I spank you for being so naughty.

"Do you think you can do something about this? What would be our best course of action?" she presses.

I rub my forehead and then the stubble on my chin. My eyes leave the file and find hers. My breath catches in my throat as I allow myself to get lost in the unique emerald color of her irises. Her lips part only a few inches from my own.

I want to kiss her. I want to make her *mine* again. Silence charged with *pure* sexual tension floods the air as we stare into each other's eyes for far longer than we should.

She stands straight, removing the tension that had settled between us. I clear my throat and loosen my tie, as it's way *too* hot in here. "You said you were from the first floor, right?"

"Yes, I'm a first-floor accounting analyst." She stands a little straighter and adjusts her blazer.

"And you have a department supervisor. Is that correct?"

Her brow furrows. "Yes, I do."

"Did you tell them of your findings?"

"I informed Mrs. Davis last night when I discovered this," she says.

"What did she say about it?" I sit back, sinking into the curves of my office chair, trying to appear in control of the situation.

I'm not.

Under my cocky facade, I'm freaking out. It's my first day as CEO, and this beautiful woman, who I fucked last night, has brought me something I have no idea how to deal with.

Tessa stands taller and straighter than I believed possible and releases a ragged breath. "She informed me that this was above my pay grade and that if I were to tell anyone else about it that it could cause undue panic, and I would be fired."

"And you decided to ignore her advice and take it straight to me?"

She nods. "Yeah, I thought it was important for you to be aware of."

"Thank you for bringing it to my attention, but I wouldn't worry your pretty little head about it. It's a screw up on the third floor, and I'm sure the proper people will take care of it."

Her eyes flash at the word *pretty*, and her body trembles. "Sorry?"

I clench my jaw. The last thing I want to do is annoy the woman I can't stop thinking about, the woman I crave. By the look on her face, I already have.

"What I mean is, you'll see that there is nothing to worry about. It will all clear itself up."

She shakes her head. "This isn't a small mistake. It is *illegal*, sir. There's no mistake. Someone here is stealing money, and I will not stand by and do nothing." Tessa reaches for the folder on top of my desk.

Without thinking, I *grip* her wrist hard, and her eyes widen as she stares at me.

"Sir, please let go of my wrist."

I narrow my eyes. "Tessa, what are you saying? Do you intend to take this information to the authorities?"

She shrugs. "I don't know. All I know is I can't work for a company that doesn't value honesty above all." She yanks her arm free and turns to leave.

My eyes land on the way her ass sways as she walks away. My cock leaks precum into my boxers.

She pauses, turning back to face me with flushed red cheeks. Damn, she looks so fucking good. "I thought you would be different. I brought this to the top, to you, because you should care about what's going on in your own company. It affects your bottom line, but I guess I was wrong. You're just like the rest of them, too lazy to deal with all the paperwork that this will incur." She shakes her head. "And, after last night…" She glances up at me, something in her eyes that I can't identify.

I want to stand up and tell her I'll look into it. I want to pull her into me and kiss her hard, but I know how unprofessional that would be. "I'm quitting, sir. Please take this as my official resignation. I can't work for a company that doesn't take matters like this seriously. This company isn't being run correctly."

That hits me in a way that makes all of my resolve snap. Rage floods my veins, heating me. "This company would run better if certain individuals would learn their place and focus on their work instead of venturing into matters above their pay *grade*."

Her fists clench, and I know I've said the wrong thing. *Shit.*

She makes me so *crazy*. I *need* to have her. "As I said, sir, please take this as my formal resignation. I shall collect my things and leave right away."

She was being serious about quitting. I thought it might have been a threat or taunt. My mind is a mess. I watch her turn and sway out of my office and out of my life.

My first day as CEO, and I know I can't make a scene, no matter how much I *want* her. At least, I know who she is now. She walks out of the room and slams the door with a forceful thud. Her feistiness only adds to the fiery need for her burning inside of me.

Charlotte rushes in, the clacking of her high-heels fills the air. "Is everything okay, sir?"

I take a long sip of water and then clear my throat, trying to process what had just happened.

"Sir? Bryson?" she asks.

I force a smile. "Of course, everything is fine." Tessa, the woman who I fucked last night, has derailed me again this afternoon. She's fearless. The way she spoke to me, no one has ever spoken to me like that before.

I want her *again* even more now. The problem is, she quit and stormed out of my office. Not to mention, it's against *every* rule in the book.

"Do you need anything else?" Charlotte asks.

"Can you order my lunch?"

"Of course." She nods and leaves.

I'm not sure what Tessa has found in the accounts. From a glance at the numbers, even I could see it didn't add up. Whatever it is, it doesn't sound good. I can't go running to my father on the first day of the job about it.

Perhaps I can theoretically run the possibility of this situation past Theo and pick his brain. From the way Tessa is acting, this is some serious shit.

8

TESSA

I rush out of Bryson's office. My entire body shakes with rage and lust, making me feel so *ashamed*.

I fucked my boss without even realizing it. What we shared last night was hot and passionate. How could I have let that asshole inside of me? I'm an idiot.

He wound me up so much I quit on the spot. I need to get out of here. This place is like all the other financial firms—full of dirty, filthy liars.

Not to mention, the CEO is very *filthy*, considering the way he spoke to me last night and the things he did to me.

I can't stop thinking about how good that man made me feel. I stand in the center of the empty elevator and wait for the doors to open. It descends from the top floor and feels like it takes *forever* to get to the first floor.

I step out of the small box and head for my office,

rushing and lamming the door behind me. I grab a stationary box and pack the entire contents of my desk and all my belongings inside the box within a few minutes.

Last night was more of a mistake than I *ever* realized. Bryson Stafford fucked me against a tree, and I haven't been able to think of anything else since. My body still *craves* his touch.

I'm not thinking about the consequence right now. I'm not thinking about how I'll afford rent or what I'll do once I've left. Bryson makes me so crazy that I don't give a shit. He wants to turn a blind eye to the fact embezzlement is taking place in his company. I can't do that.

He can deal with it himself when the feds arrive and chuck him in jail. I can't be a part of it, though.

I scoop the box up into my arms and take a moment to catch my breath. I clench my fists together so hard it feels like I might break my bones. I feel a little lightheaded as I take one last look around.

I'm already fed up with saying goodbye to places and people. The pressure in my head builds as I walk out of my office, slamming the door behind me.

A panic attack is looming over me as I head into the cramped elevator. Even though it is empty, it makes me panic. I clutch onto the box and try to focus on steadying my erratic breathing.

The box in my arms feels heavier as the elevator descends. Finally, it comes to a halt on the ground floor. I step out into the open marble entrance and let out a long, shaky breath.

The pounding in my ears is all I can hear as I walk to the front desk. I weave my way past a few people milling about in the lobby. Marlon and Anna are chatting together. Both of them look up a little surprised at me, clutching a box. "Tessa, is everything okay?" Anna asks.

I can barely reply but manage to speak. "I just quit. Here is my badge." I pass it to her.

She frowns at it. "I didn't receive any forewarning of this from upstairs."

"I told Mr. Stafford to his face. Then I went to get my things from my office and came straight here."

Anna gives me a weak smile. "Okay, do you mind if I check everything over with Mr. Stafford?"

I shake my head and tap my foot on the ground. The pounding in my head gets worse the moment Anna talks on the phone.

I grit my teeth together and try to catch my breath. Stars dance in my vision as it blurs, and before I know it, blackness ensues. The sensation of tumbling backward follows, and that's the last thing I remember.

* * *

A loud, siren-like noise fills my head as I regain consciousness. A paramedic is kneeling on the floor over me, gazing down. When I process what happened, a surge of embarrassment floods me. I passed out in the lobby of The Stafford Financial Group after quitting. I groan, trying not to let the shame overcome me.

"Miss, how are you feeling?" he asks.

I try to push myself up, but he stops me. "Careful, now, we don't know what caused you to pass out. I don't want it happening again. Could you look this way for me?" He points to the right as he shines a light into my eyes. Once he withdraws the blinding light, I watch him nod with satisfaction.

"All right, let's get you up," he says.

I rest a hand on his arm as he helps me to my feet. He directs me to a bench in the middle of the lobby and asks me some questions about my medical history, which I run through.

A familiar and irritating voice echoes through the lobby, "Go about your business. There is nothing to see here."

Bryson Stafford.

He approaches me and stands towering over us. I want to punch him right now and kiss him. My feelings toward this man I fucked last night are so mixed up. He's the reason I fainted. He's the reason I no longer have a job.

"What's the verdict?" he asks.

The paramedic stands and faces him. "She will be fine. I think it was a panic attack that overwhelmed her and led to a momentary lapse of consciousness. The security guard caught her, so she didn't hit her head."

Bryson smiles at the paramedic. "Thank you for taking care of my employee. I'll take it from here."

The paramedic nods and then grabs his equipment. I

don't want to be anywhere near Bryson right now. Yet, here he is, smiling at me.

The son of a bitch learned I had a panic attack and passed out, and he's looking like the cat who got the damn cream. Once the paramedic is gone, he takes a seat next to me—closer than I'd like.

"Are you okay?" Bryson asks.

I shake my head. "I'm fine. If you would leave me alone, I'd greatly appreciate it, *sir*." I say the last word mockingly as it's not like he is my boss any more.

"Why were you handing in your name badge?" he asks.

My brow furrows. "I told you. I quit. There is *no way* I'm working for this company a moment longer."

He laughs in a way that makes me grit my teeth together. "I thought you were just angry. Surely, we can discuss this like adults." His blue eyes flash with playfulness. He knows he's suggesting I'm acting like a child, and it only angers me more.

"I'm not working for you or this company for a moment longer. There is nothing to discuss."

Bryson sighs and runs a hand through his dark brown hair. "I may have said some things back there that I didn't mean." He shuffles on the bench, moving closer to me. "I'm under a lot of pressure at the moment." There is genuine turmoil in his tone, and I'm surprised to see him looking so vulnerable for a moment, considering he is the acting CEO of this company.

"I can't turn a blind eye to what is going on here. It's wrong."

"Good, you're the kind of woman I need on my side. I will get my driver to take you home so you can rest for a little while and then get dressed. He will take you to a restaurant where we will have an early dinner and discuss everything you learned. Okay?"

The way he stares into my eyes makes the hair on the back of my neck stand on end. All I can remember as I look at him is the way it felt when he took me against that tree. My thighs quiver. I know going to a restaurant with him is a bad idea, as my body doesn't seem to hate him as much as my mind does.

I want to say no to him. He's so cocky and demanding. "Fine." I stand up. "I'll see you later."

He stands and grabs my hand in his. I glance around, wondering if anyone is going to see the CEO acting so unprofessional with me, but no one seems to bat an eyelid. "Let me walk you out."

I sigh and tear my hand from his. "Fine." I move to grab my box, but before I can, he scoops it up into his strong arms.

"I'll take the box. You don't want to pass out again from overexerting yourself."

I think he knows how much he is annoying me right now. I huff and then march toward the door. I still can't believe I fucked this asshole last night. Last night, he was a different man, kind and attentive.

Bryson follows me out into the busy street, but I don't wait for him. I'm not even sure where I'm going until a young man steps up toward me. "Tessa Clayton?" he asks.

I nod in response.

"I'm Tom, and the car is over here." I glance back to see Bryson looking irritated, trying to fight his way through the bustling bodies, chasing behind me.

"Bryson, I'll take that for you." Tom grabs the box and bundles it into the black limo in front of us.

My heart skips a beat as Bryson's hands settle on my hips, sending heat flooding through my veins. His warm breath tickles my exposed neck as he leans down to whisper in my ear. "I'll see you later, Tessa." His voice is deep and husky. He pulls me even closer to him, and I feel his thick, long cock pressing into my backside, making me *moan*. "Don't stand me up."

I want this man again. It's ridiculous. I don't like Bryson, but I want him.

Despite myself, my panties are dripping wet already. The way he acted earlier over the embezzlement scheme was infuriating.

But I can't shake the way his body feels pressed against mine. How good it felt when he made me come all over his face or with his cock buried deep inside of me. My body responds in a way I *wish* it wouldn't. I can't deny the truth. My body wants him as badly as my mind dislikes him.

He presses a kiss against my shoulder, trailing up my neck before disappearing into the crowd.

I glance back to get a glimpse of him, but he is gone. This is a bad idea. It seems my body is not listening to reason, especially after last night.

Bryson Stafford is the worst kind of man imaginable. So why the hell are my panties so wet?

9

BRYSON

I try to stop thinking about Tessa for the next hour, throwing myself into work to keep my mind busy. If her findings are correct, then my company is embroiled in an embezzlement scandal.

I may not be the brightest financial mind, but even I could see that. It's a damn miracle no one has picked up on it before and taken it straight to the authorities. Somehow, I need to get to the bottom of it without bringing scandal on the company.

The pressure of an oncoming headache between my eyes is starting as I rub my forehead. The stress is getting to me already. I walk down the hallway toward my brother's office. The squeak of my leather brogues across the polished marble breaks the silence. This afternoon, I've been pacing so much my feet are numb and tired. I walk around the corner to the back office, where my brother should be working.

I draw in a deep breath as I come to a stop outside his door. Is this the right thing to do? I know how dangerous it is to risk admitting to my brother that this is happening while I'm in charge. I don't intend to tell him outright. If I make it hypothetical, I may get away with it. I knock on his door.

"Come in," Theo says.

I open the door, letting myself in. Theo glances up at me. His eyes widen when he sees me standing in his doorway.

"Brother, how can I help you?" Theo drums his fingers on the desk.

I stand there a moment in silence as Theo stares up at me. My mind is still a scrambled mess, and as I glance at my watch, I haven't got long until my reservation for dinner with Tessa.

Even her name excites me more than it should. My cock hardens at the image of her beautifully flushed cheeks earlier. I shake my head and try to push the mental picture out of my mind, returning my attention to Theo, who is scowling at me now. "What is it, brother? Spit it out."

"I want to ask you what you would do in a hypothetical situation."

Theo's brow raises, but he nods and gestures for me to take a seat. "Okay, take a seat."

I move to take a seat in front of my brother's desk. He cocks his head to the side as he stares at me. "It's unlike you to ask my opinion."

I shrug. "I heard someone discussing something that happened at another firm. The guy stumbled upon an embezzlement scheme. It got me thinking about if that were to happen within our company. I mean, as CEO, you need to be ready for any and every situation, right?" I ask.

Theo nods. "Yes, what did you hear?"

"As far as I could gather, their company set up some health and wellness accounts instead of making everyone have to buy insurance. The money they were taking out of the employee's paychecks was siphoned into other areas of the company, rather than being used to pay for the employee's benefits. Even though the employees have been told that they can access the money, they haven't seen a cent."

Theo's eyes widen. "Is there a company doing this now?"

"No, I heard some guys talking today while we were waiting on Mr. Gates. And, they were talking about how a company did it a few years back. They're not doing it now."

I can't risk Theo learning this was going on right now. It could blow my entire quarter in charge out of the water.

Theo wipes the phantom sweat from his brow. "Well, if you were to hear our competition doing it, then you would need to go to the authorities because if they suspect you know something, they will be on your back. The IRS will come down hard on anyone involved."

"I know. I guess that's why it rattled me. If something like that were to be brought to our attention here, how would a CEO go about dealing with it?"

Theo raises a brow as a moment of silence passes between them. "Well, the proper thing to do in this situation is to investigate in house. This way, you don't alert those who are involved, making them bolt. There's no need for unwanted and unflattering publicity, which not only makes you look bad but destroys all future trust in the company. Ultimately, losing the company billions of dollars, as customers will go to the competition instead."

I nod. "That makes sense. I feel like I have so much to learn about being a CEO." I rest my head in my hands.

I intend to get a certain woman to help me with a quiet investigation.

Tessa.

She seems bright. She was the first person to catch onto the scheme. She's the only person I can trust, considering she attempted to quit because of her morals.

Theo, to my surprise, stands and rests a hand on my shoulder. "Don't worry, brother. You'll get there. Both of us will." He smiles. "I'm not sure why our father doesn't make us joint CEOs. It would make it easier for both of us."

I can't deny I'm surprised by his sentiment. "Why don't you suggest it to him?"

"I have. Dad insisted that The Stafford Financial Group has always had one CEO and always will."

I sigh. "I wish he would consider it. We'd do better

running this place together." My heart sinks, as it would make everything so much easier.

Theo knows finance better than me, and he would do a good job, but he lacks the management skills that I possess. I want to prove I can step up to the mark.

"We're brothers, not enemies. I don't enjoy fighting against you." Theo walks toward the wall and grabs something from the side. "No matter what happens. If you win or I win, it won't make a difference. We will both still work here together." He smiles at me.

I can't help but smile back. "May the best man win."

"Which is me," Theo says, smirking.

"Bullshit."

Theo laughs and then glances at the clock. "Right, I've got a meeting with the Johnson firm, so if that's all…"

"Of course." I stand from the chair. "Thank you for listening."

He winks. "Anytime, big brother."

I let myself out of his office, relieved at how easy that was. I'd expected him to probe me more. Tom should be on the way to the restaurant with Tessa already. It's almost six o'clock. I'd ordered another car to wait for me outside. After speaking with my brother, my proposal to Tessa is the right move. I'm going to ask her to come back to The Stafford Financial Group as my financial advisor. She can help me tackle the embezzlement issue, and I can address my *obsession* with the woman.

It's wrong to want to sleep with my employee again.

Well, former employee, who I intend to win back onto my side tonight at dinner.

I march out into the street. The black town car I ordered is waiting for me. Tom will already be on his way to the restaurant with Tessa. It's ridiculous that I have butterflies beating around in my stomach at the mere thought of her *name*.

The woman who could help me figure out what was happening in my company. Hopefully, she can help me with something else too. I glance down at my tenting pants. *Fuck*. I know how unprofessional it is to want to be balls deep in my employee again.

It's a sure-fire way to piss my father off. A CEO can't get involved with an employee. It's against everything he has ever taught me. Not to mention, it breaks every sexual conduct rule in the damn rule book.

10

TESSA

"Holy *shit*." The door slams shut. "There's some fancy limo parked right outside the apartment *block*," Elena shouts.

I've kept Tom waiting for longer than I should have. Bryson told me I could rest up and then get dressed, but I've been in here an hour and a half. I've changed my outfit about ten times, and I don't even know why.

That's a lie. I know why—because I want to fuck Bryson *again*, even though I shouldn't.

Bryson Stafford is taking me to dinner to discuss business, and I'm panicking over what to wear. I shouldn't care how I look. "Yeah, I know. It's waiting for *me*," I shout back.

"No freaking *way*." Her footsteps echo toward my bedroom. "What's going on?"

I sigh, and her eyes travel up and down my body. "Wow, you look amazing."

I can feel my cheeks heating. "Thanks, do you think so?" I twirl to look in the mirror behind me.

It's the *sixth* dress I've tried on. A burgundy maxi dress showing a little more cleavage than I usually would. I know it's because I *want* Bryson again. Even after our argument in his office, I can't forget the way his lips felt on mine or the way it felt when his huge cock plunged deeper inside of me than any man has *ever* been.

"Yeah, you look *hot*. What's the occasion?"

I turn and glance at my friend. "You know the man from last night at the bar?"

She twirls her hair in her fingers. "Of course."

"Well, I didn't realize until today that he is my boss, Bryson Stafford."

Her mouth falls open. "Fuck me. Are you serious?"

"Yep, and I quit my job when he wouldn't take the embezzlement thing seriously."

Her eyes widen. "What?"

I hold my hand up. "I know, then Bryson asked me to go to dinner with him to discuss it tonight. He says he was shocked and wants to discuss how to fix it. Right now I'm in limbo, to be honest. I'm not sure what will happen."

She shakes her head. "Wow, that is crazy."

"I know. The guy in the limo is his driver, and I've been taking forever to decide what to wear," I say.

Elena's eyebrow rises. "Because you like your boss?"

I shake my head, feeling heat flood me. I was too ashamed of what I did last night to tell her. It was so out of character for me. "No, he's a corporate, cocky asshole."

"That's not what you said about him last night." Her eyebrow raises.

I told her last night we kissed, and that I enjoyed it. She's right. Before I knew he was Bryson Stafford, I couldn't stop thinking about him.

Elena rushes toward my closet and digs around, searching for something. "You've got to wear these shoes. They go perfect with that dress." She pulls out a pair of black high heels that I haven't worn since before I moved in with her.

I smile. "I don't know if I even remember how to walk in heels that high."

"Don't be silly. Try them on." She holds them out, walking toward me.

I take them from her and put them on, checking if they look good in the mirror. "Okay, they go well with this outfit." I twirl around once more. I grab my bag off the bed and slinging it over my shoulder. "Wish me luck."

"Good luck," Elena says, jumping up and pulling me into a quick hug.

I sigh and head out the door. Tom is leaning against the hood of the limo, tapping his foot on the sidewalk. He smiles as he sees me. "Ready, Miss?"

"Yes, I'm so sorry I took so long."

He shrugs. "No problem at all. Get settled in, and I'll have you at the restaurant in no time."

My stomach twists at the thought. Am I ready to sit at

a dinner table with my boss? I slide into the leather seat in the back and rest my head in my hands.

All I can think about is our heated session in the park last night. There is no way I'm going to be able to focus on the important task at hand with him sitting across from me. He may be cocky, but he's the hottest man I've *ever* met.

* * *

The limo ride seems to go on forever. Finally, Tom pulls the car to a stop and winds down the screen. "We're here, miss. I will check in with the boss and find out if he's here yet. Sit tight."

"Okay, thank you, Tom."

He smiles back at me before winding the screen up.

I fidget as I sit, waiting for what feels like forever. After a while, the door to the limo swings open, but it's not Tom opening the door.

Bryson's stunning face appears at the opening. His bright blue eyes are twinkling. "Sorry, I was a little late." He holds out his hand for me to take.

I shuffle over and place my feet on the floor before taking his hand. I allow him to help me out onto the sidewalk in front of the swankiest restaurant in Wynton.

My heart beats against my rib cage, as Bryson sets a kiss against my cheek. It's innocent enough, but the thoughts I have when he gets that close are far from innocent. "You look stunning this evening," he whispers in my ear.

The hair on the back of my neck stands on end and

my throbbing pussy drips. How does this man have so much power over my body?

"Thank you." I run my eyes over the fancy tux he is wearing. "You don't look *too* bad yourself."

His smile widens, and I think I've just inflated his ego, which didn't need boosting. Especially not if all the stories I've read about him are *true*. That he's a womanizing playboy who doesn't pay any regard to women's feelings, and I fucked him last night. The type of man I should stay miles away from, especially after Ted.

Will I ever learn?

I *groan* to myself internally. It seems I won't as I walk into the restaurant on the arm of a man who is bad news.

"Bryson Stafford, please come this way," the front of house says as soon as he notices him.

We follow the man through the busy restaurant right to the back. He seats us at a private booth. It's the perfect place to discuss the sensitive topic of embezzlement in his company. I sit down first, and Bryson slides in next to me and closer than I want. My stomach lurches as he sets his hand on my thigh.

I bat away his hand and shift further from him. "Sir, I thought you asked me here to discuss the serious matter of embezzlement at the company." I frown at him.

It doesn't seem to deter him as he shuffles closer to me. "We are, but I'd also like to get to know you better, Tessa."

The way he says my name sends a wave of need

through me. I need to get a hold of my urges. Otherwise, I'm going to end up doing something I regret with my boss again. "Do you realize how inappropriate that is?" I shake my head. "You're the acting CEO of the company that employs me, or employed me."

His face turns serious. "I still regard you as an employee."

A sense of relief flutters through me to hear I'm not unemployed. It depends on how this meeting goes, whether I want to stay at The Stafford Financial Group. "I'm not sure I want to stay."

"I know I said some offensive things back in my office." His face turns serious. "The information you brought to me shocked me. The fact is, Tessa, you're the only one that can help me right now. And I'm desperate."

I shake my head. "That makes no sense. Why would you, the CEO of Stafford Financial, need the help of a first-floor accounting analyst?"

He cocks his head to the side. "I'll be open with you. I know how important that is."

I nod and wait for him to continue.

"My father is allowing me to run the company for three months." He clears his throat. "After which, he intends to let my brother take over for three months. It's a trial period, you see. My father wants to ensure he leaves the most capable person in control."

Bryson pauses and takes in a deep breath. "If I bring this up with my father, then I risk proving to him I'm not capable. However, if you will work with me." He flashes me a panty-melting smile. "And help me sort this out, then I can prove that I can avoid a crisis and fix problems."

I nod, processing what he said. "I understand you don't want to rush to your father, but surely, he would understand with something this *big*? It's something that could destroy the entire company with scandal."

Bryson runs a hand through his hair. "My father is unwell." He swallows hard. "This is confidential, but we don't know how long he has left."

A sudden urge to comfort him washes over me, and I set a hand over his. "I'm so sorry, Bryson."

He gazes into my eyes and forces a sad smile. "Thank you." He lets out a deep sigh. "I've often let down my father in my life. Let's say I've not made good choices in the past. He's been ashamed of me most of the time. My last chance to make him proud. I've got to…" He trails off, his eyes filling with tears. He clears his throat again. "The way you acted earlier proved to me you value honesty above all. I can trust you with this. At least, I hope I can." He shuts his eyes.

"Of course." I reach out for his hand again and squeeze. "You can trust me."

"I can't afford for this to get out. I just can't." His words are passionate, and they heat me in ways it shouldn't.

I'm surprised how much it means to him to make his father proud, especially after everything I'd heard about Bryson Stafford.

"I understand. I won't tell anyone, although…"

Bryson's eyebrow raises. "What is it?"

"Total honesty, right?" I clarify.

He nods.

"I told my roommate about it last night." I bite my lip. "I couldn't keep it to myself. After Mrs. Davis threatened my job, I needed to vent. I told her before we spoke at the bar."

He smiles. "I assume you can trust your friend not to share this information?"

"Yeah, Elena would never tell anyone."

He lets out a long sigh. "How about we order some food and try not to think about this right now? We'll dive into this more tomorrow morning at the office if you agree to help me."

Before I can even respond, Bryson has called a waiter over. "What can I get you, sir?"

"A bottle of your best champagne. Also, a fillet steak, medium, with the pepper sauce." He glances at me. "What would you like?"

"I'll have the duck, please."

He smiles at me as the waiter leaves. "What do you think about helping me out, then? I want to bring you back on as my financial advisor." His blue eyes sparkle in the lights of the restaurant.

"Financial advisor?" I shake my head. "I'm not qualified for that position. I'm an accounting analyst. But I will help you with this issue and then return to my position afterward," I say.

His smile widens, and the tension leaves his shoulders.

"I need to lay some ground rules first," I say.

He sits back in the chair and stares at me. "Of course."

"I will need to access everything," I say.

"Agreed."

"Also, this could get messy. You may learn things about people you know well and believe are incapable of doing wrong. No matter who turns out to be in on this, I need you to promise you won't try to sweep it under the carpet." I stare at him. "If you try anything, then I'll have no choice but to take it above your head."

"I promise I won't, no matter what." Bryson shuffles closer to me. He takes my hand in his. "Shall we shake hands?"

A tingling sensation rushes through my body at his touch. All I can think about is the way this man felt inside of me last night.

I nod and shake his hand, but he doesn't let go right away. It's only once the waiter returns with our champagne and pours us each a glass that he lets go. I take the drink, thankful for the distraction from the palpable tension between us.

11

BRYSON

I sit *closer* to Tessa than I should. As the champagne flows, the conversation does too. It's natural as we chat like we did the night before. This time she's asking me more questions, and I answer her.

Normally, I don't tell people anything about me, but I can't deny this woman anything. Her laugh is as beautiful as the rest of her. I can't help but feel drawn to her even more, memories of our passionate sex the night before flashing through my mind. It makes my balls ache for release.

I could spend *all* my time with her and never get bored. It's a first for me to feel this way.

My cock throbs in my pants. I've sat here the entire night with a hard-on. She's not making it easy on me in that sexy dress. The way her perfect, pert breasts are exposed to me makes me *crazy*. I'm desperate for this woman.

She bats her eyelashes innocently as she takes another swig of champagne. She's anything but innocent if last night is anything to go on. Her cheeks are flushed a pretty pink.

I can't hold back any longer. I shuffle closer to her and take her hand in my own. Her eyes widen, but her lips part, showing she isn't opposed to my advances.

I pull her toward me, and our lips crash in a hard, desperate kiss. She tastes of champagne and her own sweet taste. I *groan* into her mouth, clawing at her. My cock jumps in my pants as I press my thigh against hers.

Her body melts into me as she moans into my mouth. Her hand snakes onto my thigh, digging her fingertips into me. I place my hand on her thigh and let it move higher and higher toward her dripping wet arousal, letting my fingers tease over the wet fabric of her thong.

Tessa hesitates as her hand on my thigh pauses inches from my rock-hard cock. I want her to touch it and feel her small hands on my length again.

I deepen the kiss, plundering her mouth with my tongue, and dip my finger into her slick, wet lips. She moans *louder* than she should, moving her hand to cup my throbbing cock. I growl as precum leaks from the swollen crown into my boxer briefs.

Her hands feel my fabric clad length, feeling every inch of me. I kiss her again, capturing her lips as I thrust my thick finger in and out of her pussy. She tenses up and shuffles away, forcing my finger from her.

"What's wrong?" I ask.

She shakes her head. Her lips open slightly. "We can't... I can't..." She's speechless as she gazes up at me.

"Tell me, baby."

She grits her teeth together. "Don't call me that. Mr. Stafford, we're supposed to be professionals, discussing a delicate issue. We can't let what happened between us get in the way."

My stomach dips.

She shakes her head again. "We can't be intimate. You're the CEO of the company I work for, and we're investigating an embezzlement scheme together."

I lick my lips. "Your point is?" I raise an eyebrow.

"My point is we need to make sure we keep this professional." She points between the two of us.

I sigh. My cock is not in agreement at all. It wants nothing more than to be buried to the hilt inside of her again. I can feel my precum spilling into my boxers. I'm harder than steel.

"Whatever you want," I say through gritted teeth, as I grab the bottle of champagne and pour her the last glass.

She tries to protest. "Sir, what about you?"

"Enjoy the last glass, Tessa. If you'll excuse me, I need to use the bathroom. Then, when you're ready, we'll leave."

She nods, and I can almost feel her eyes tracking me across the room. I need to take care of this hard-on before I *come* in my pants. I head into the bathroom, which to my relief is empty, and let myself into a stall. I free my hard cock as fast as I can, fisting it into my hand.

My eyes shut as I picture Tessa's beautiful pink lips wrapped around it, just like last night.

She's *all* I want. Why is she fighting the inevitable? We've already fucked, so what's stopping her?

I know she didn't know who I was last night, while I sunk every thick inch inside her. I fist my cock, grunting as I tighten my grip and remember just how good she felt.

This woman makes me crazy. I was on the verge of fucking her there in the restaurant. Around Tessa, I lose control of all of my senses. She drives me *wild*. She's out there on her own, waiting for me while I jerk off over her. It is so perverted and filthy. I should be fucking her instead.

My eyes shut, and the image of Tessa's full lips wrapping around my head, flash behind my eyelids. I remember the way she took my dick into her throat. It was damn sexy.

Fuck.

I want to bend her over my desk and plow into her hard, her naked, curvy form, bending to my will as I slap her full ass. The image of my cock sinking deep into her tight, wet pussy as she bends over my desk is fucking hot.

I need her so badly. My balls clench, I grunt as much needed release washes through me, and I shoot rope after rope of cum into the bowl below.

The sound of the door to the men's room opening startles me, and I shove my softening dick back into my pants before letting myself out of the cubicle and washing my hands. I stroll toward Tessa, who is waiting for me.

I wonder how long I was in the bathroom. Would it be obvious that I just jerked off in there? I slide into the booth and smile at her. "Sorry for keeping you waiting. Where were we?" I ask.

I know where we were before she pulled away. Her hand had been gloriously parked on my cock. Her cheeks redden even more. "I think you said once I'm ready that we will leave, sir."

How am I supposed to keep my hands to myself in the back of the limo? "Are you ready?"

She nods. "I can get a cab if you—"

I silence her, holding my hand in the air. "No chance. I'll drop you home." I stand and throw down four hundred dollars, knowing it's more than enough to cover our meal. She stares at the cash with wide eyes.

I hold out an arm for her to take. "Let's go."

She takes my arm and allows me to escort her out of the restaurant. Tom is waiting for us at the front and opens the door to my limo to allow us in. I hold Tessa's hand as she slides into the back of the limo.

I turn to Tom once she's out of earshot. "Can you keep the privacy screen up, please?"

Tom gives me a knowing wink. "No problem, sir."

I slide in next to Tessa, closer than she would like, as she shifts away. She turns to face me. "What is the plan for the investigation?"

"As soon as you arrive tomorrow morning, come

straight to my office on the top floor." I run a hand through my hair. "We will start straight away."

She nods and sits back in the leather chair, letting out a long breath.

I shift toward her. "What's wrong?"

She shakes her head. "Nothing, I can't believe I stumbled on such a huge scheme going on in the company I work for." She swallows hard.

"Neither can I. I won't deny your timing sucks, and that's why I acted like a dick earlier. It's my first day of acting CEO, and I'm under a lot of stress as it is, anyway."

She gazes up at me.

"What I'm trying to say is, I'm sorry for the way I acted earlier."

She smiles at me. "Apology accepted."

We gaze into each other's eyes for so long I'm sure I can feel electricity surging in the air between us. She licks her lips, and I can't stop myself. I move toward, placing my lips against hers tentatively.

She tenses for a moment before she relaxes into it, moaning as my tongue caresses her mouth with all the desire I possess for her.

She straddles my lap, letting her hot, thong-clad pussy rest against my bulge. I can feel the wet patch her panties are making on my suit pants, and it turns me on. I groan, gripping her hips tighter. Even though I dealt with my hard-on less than ten minutes ago, my cock is thick and throbbing against her, pressing between her thighs.

She grinds against me, making more precum leak into my boxers. I kiss her more deeply as she tries to find friction against my cock. It drives me wild with need. I grab her thighs and move my hands up her hips, lifting the skirt of her dress to expose her wet panties.

Tessa is lost in her desire, gazing at me with lust-filled eyes. My fingers make their way to her pussy, and I gasp at how soaking wet she is. Ever wetter than at the restaurant or last night, she's dripping for me.

"Fuck, your naughty pussy is so wet thinking about my thick cock."

She grinds even harder into me. "We shouldn't be doing this," she gasps.

I grab her ass cheeks possessively. "Come back to my place."

She worries her bottom lip between her teeth. "We shouldn't."

I take the one night only approach, even though I know I'll *want* her again. "Tessa, my desire for you needs to be quenched, and from how fucking wet you are, you need it too. Let's give in to that desire, just for tonight. It will make it easier going forward for both of us."

She searches my eyes for a moment before nodding her head. I groan, kissing her full, plump lips and then smiling against them.

I press the intercom in the back of the limo. "Tom?"
"Yes, sir?"
"Can you take us straight back to my place, please?"
"Of course, sir. I'll turn around right now."

I dip my finger right back inside her tight, wet pussy, and she moans. "I'm going to make you come all over my fingers before we even get back to my apartment, Tessa," I growl, kissing her neck and then biting down on her collarbone.

She *cries* out, trying to stifle the sound with her teeth.

"Come here," I command, gripping her hips and forcing her to lie over my lap. "Naughty girls get punished. Would you like me to punish you, baby?"

She nods, gazing back at me with lust-filled eyes. I ease her panties down, exposing her beautiful ass cheeks to my hungry gaze. I slap her ass, making her moan. A pink mark spread across her cheek as I slap the other cheek, making her gasp.

"Do you enjoy having your ass slapped?"

"Yes, sir," she moans, grinding her clit against my thigh to get friction. I slip my fingers between her wet lips and dip them right into the knuckle. All *three*.

She bucks her hips and gasps as I plunge my fingers in and out of her. The wet noise her pussy makes is like music to my ears, and I can't wait to feel her around my cock.

I slap her ass with my free hand, making her whimper. "Do you like me punishing you, Tessa?" I groan, rubbing the pink flesh of her ass. "Do you like your boss slapping your ass?"

She glances back at me and nods. "I like it, sir."

I growl, as hearing her call me sir drives me wild. I pull my fingers from her pussy, and she whimpers. I turn her over and force her to sit on my lap, pulling her lips to mine in a hard kiss.

"Open your mouth, baby," I groan.

She does as I say, and I slide my fingers slick with her juice inside. "Taste your own sweet pussy like a good girl."

She hums around my fingers, licking them clean.

"On your hands and knees." I rub my cock through my pants.

She does as I say, sticking her ass up in the air and inviting me. I let my tongue tease at her dripping wet folds, tasting the sweet juice dripping from her. She tastes even better than I remember as I let my tongue flick against her clit.

"Bryson," she whimpers, arching her back more.

I slap her ass cheeks and then grab her hips, pulling her pussy even tighter to me. I dip my tongue deep inside of her and taste as much of as her as I can. I circle her clit with my finger, as I use my tongue to fuck her dripping wet pussy.

Her hips buck and writhe as I drag her higher and higher toward the point of no return. I need her to come all over my face and drench my tongue in her honeyed juice. I move away, still rubbing her clit with my fingers. "I want you to come on my face, Tessa," I growl, my breath teasing against her wet lips.

She nods her head.

I return my mouth to her lips, sucking at them gently with my mouth before plunging my tongue back inside her dripping heat. My fingers tease her sensitive nub more and more, making the pressure build as my tongue plunges in and out of her.

"Bryson," she gasps as her muscles clamp around me, and she releases. Her body convulses against me as she spills her sweet cum onto my tongue.

I growl, lapping up every drop. I don't stop until I've got all of it, and she is slumped over, spent from her orgasm. I pull her into my lap and kiss her.

Something tells me this is going to be a *very* long night.

12

TESSA

Bryson claws at me like an animal in heat as he pushes me through his apartment door. I barely have a moment to glance around it, and he's crashing into me *hard*.

His muscled body presses into me. His thick cock is straining against my abdomen. "Strip," he growls, sending a needy heat pulsing through my body.

I vowed not to do this. I don't like Bryson Stafford. He's a cocky, rich asshole who thinks he can have whatever he wants. Yet, here I am, pulling my dress off over my head as he watches me with the fierce, possessive gaze heating his deep blue eyes.

I need him. He's all I can think about ever since we fucked. Maybe this will ease that heat. Maybe having sex in his apartment won't be as hot, and it will get him out of my mind.

He unbuttons his shirt, watching me unhook my bra and freeing my full breasts to his gaze. A low growl rumbles through his chest, and his eyes heat more at the sight of my peaked nipples, pointing right at him.

The breath catches in my throat as he eases the shirt off his muscled body. He's more ripped than I'd ever imagined — six-foot-four of pure hard muscle and abs that make my mouth water. I want to touch every inch of him, worship him.

His fingers move to the belt of his pants, and he eases it off as I hook a finger into the waistband of my lacy thong, pulling it down.

I stand in front of my boss, naked and exposed, watching as he eases his pants down. His huge, thick cock is *bulging* inside his tight boxer briefs. A wet patch at the tip where he's been leaking precum. I lick my lips at the thought of tasting him again.

He eases the waistband of his boxer briefs down, and his rock-hard length slaps against his abs. My eyes widen in disbelief. I knew he was big. I felt just how big when he fucked me, but in the low light of the park with our clothes still on, I didn't see just how *huge* he was. It's a beautiful sight. The thick, swollen head coated in pearly precum.

I drop to my knees and take him into my mouth, desperate to taste him again. He *groans* above me, threading his rough fingers through my hair. My small hands circle the thick base of his cock, unable to reach all the way around. I suck on the head, drawing every drop of precum out and into my mouth before closing my lips around him.

I bob my head up and down, taking more of him into my throat than I did last night. It's hard to believe that it's been twenty-four hours since I lost my mind and gave myself to this man in public. I cup his heavy, cum-filled balls in my hands. He growls, moving his muscled hips and rocking his cock deeper into my throat.

I relax my gag reflex and let him fuck my throat. It's an exciting and freeing sensation, giving up control to this powerful man standing above me. My nose hits his lower abdomen as every long, thick inch slips into my throat.

"Fuck, Tessa," he growls, pulling back and letting his cock spring from my mouth.

I whimper at the loss of him, wanting to taste every hot, salty drop of his cum. "I want you to cum down my throat," I moan, gazing into his eyes.

They flash fiercely, and he grips hold of my hair. "That's such a dirty thing to say, Tessa. You want to swallow every drop of my cum, do you?"

I nod, shocked at how wanton this man makes me. "Yes, please, sir."

He growls, shoving his thick cock between my lips and forcing every inch back down my throat. He roars as he unleashes his cum to the back of my mouth, splash after splash slides down my throat, coating it in his cum. He pulls back slightly as the cum keeps spilling onto my tongue, making my pussy gush at the sweet, masculine taste of him inside my mouth. I hum around his cock as I clean every last drop off, making sure I've swallowed *all* of his seed.

He pulls me up by my hair and crashes his mouth into mine, tasting himself. "Fuck, Tessa. You make me so crazy," he growls, fisting his still hard cock in his hand. "My turn to taste your sweet pussy, baby."

He grabs hold of my hips and forces me backward until I drop onto a sofa. "Lie back, baby girl. I'm going to make you come so hard you'll be begging me to fuck you."

I bite my bottom lip hard and watch him as he moves toward me, fisting his length in his hands. I can't quite believe I'm doing this with my boss.

What the hell am I thinking?

He kneels in front of me, and I feel his hot breath teasing against my clit. All reasoning is gone again. He flicks his tongue out against my hard, throbbing nub, making me buck toward him. His large, rough hands pin me to the sofa, and he licks me right from my clit, parting my lips. He doesn't stop there, though, and I gasp as his tongue swirls around my asshole. It's so *filthy*, but it makes me wetter than ever.

"That's it, baby. Let me lick that beautiful fucking asshole."

I moan, enjoying the forbidden, thrilling pleasure of his tongue teasing me there.

He drags his tongue back through my dripping wet lips and then circles my clit again, teasingly. He thrusts three thick fingers deep inside my pussy, making my back arch.

He thrust in and out, building the pressure within seconds. I've already come in the back of his limo, but he brings me right back to the edge so fucking quickly. I moan as he sucks my hard clit into his mouth, making my pussy ache for more. His fingers feel good, but I need his cock deep inside of me.

"Fuck me," I moan, threading my fingers in his dark, thick hair.

He gazes up at me, still licking and sucking at the sensitive bundle of nerves. He shakes his head and then grazes his teeth over my clit. That's all it takes for me to explode onto his fingers. They clamp down hard around him, and I scream his name over and over again. My orgasm is rocking through me so intensely white filters into my vision.

"Now, I'm going to fuck you," He growls, shifting from the sofa and crawling over me, letting his thick, swollen cock bump against my aching clit.

"Please, Bryson… Please." He captures my lips, kissing me hard.

I let my hands roam his hard, muscled chest as he pulls back and gazes at me. His thick, long cock rests at my entrance, ready to take me. I'm shaking with needy desire for him.

"Is this what you want, Tessa? My cock stretching that hungry little *cunt* and making it come again?"

I nod my head, unable to speak. I'm too desperate for him.

He pushes his muscled hips forward. Inch after inch of his shaft disappears inside of me, making me moan *deeply.*

The pressure builds the moment his thick, throbbing length stretches me like I've *craved* ever since last night. He moves slowly this time, watching me as I take his cock all the way in and his balls rest against my ass.

His eyes heat with desire. It's slow and hard as he pulls back until only the throbbing crown is inside of me, and then he slides back in with one quick thrust.

I *cry* out at the sensation, wishing he'd fuck me harder. I need to feel him *taking* me the way he did last night, against that tree.

"Harder," I moan.

Bryson bites my lip between his teeth and growls. "Dirty girl. You want me to fuck you hard like I did last night, don't you?"

I nod my head, clawing at his wide shoulders as he pulls his cock out of me, leaving me empty and needy.

He thrusts right back in, his balls slapping against my ass. I cry out, feeling him fill me so deep it feels like there's no more room inside of me. He's filling me and stretching me. The heat rushing through me is beyond anything I've ever felt.

He captures my lips with his own, kissing me hard and passionately. I shouldn't be fucking my boss, but I *need* this. I *need* him. The reasonable side of me is screaming how wrong this is, but it's drowned out by my primal and wanton part of me that longs for this man to fuck me all night long.

"Fuck me," I moan, clawing at his back, trying to get him deeper inside of me.

Bryson growls, gripping hold of my hips and pulling out of me. "On your hands and knees, baby."

I do as he says, shaking as I turn over. His thick cock thrusts back inside of me in one hard motion, making me scream in pleasure. He grunts above me as he fucks me harder and faster, drawing that perfect pleasure from deep within me. My pussy is aching for release as he drills me so perfectly.

His fingers find my throbbing, swollen clit, and he rubs me in a way that sets me on fire. How does this man do these things to me? I'm twenty-five years old. I've had my fair share of boyfriends, and no man has ever done what this man does to me. It's on another level: Earth-Shattering and groundbreaking.

"Bryson," I moan his name, getting lost in the heat of it.

"That's it, Tessa. Moan my name while I fuck you."

I'm teetering on the edge of an orgasm, my whole body ready to take off like a damn rocket.

He thrust into me hard and fast from behind, hitting the spot inside of me that makes my toes curl. Our bodies moving together fill the room with wet noises as my pussy drips everywhere.

The muscles around his cock tighten and tense as he holds me on edge, stilling inside of me. I whimper at the sudden stillness.

"I want to watch your face as you come for me," he growls, lifting me and sitting down on the sofa with me. "Turn around and face me."

I ease myself off his cock, shaking as I straddle his thick thighs. He kisses me as I impale myself on his huge shaft, moaning at the full sensation.

"Ride my cock, baby," he groans, lowering his head to suck my aching, hard nipple into his mouth.

It builds the pressure right back up inside of me as I bob up and down on his cock, riding him harder and faster.

His fingers dip into my hips, and he helps ease me up and down his length, holding my gaze. One hand snakes between us, and he teases my clit, pushing me closer to climax. It's rushing toward me with unprecedented force.

"Come for me, Tessa. I want to feel you come all over my cock."

I throw my head back as pure ecstasy shoots through my nerves, lighting my entire body on fire. I writhe above him, still grinding against him as he thrust his hips up to meet my movements.

He roars against my lips as he unleashes his seed deep inside of me, pumping his hips again and again. I can feel our mingled juices running down my thighs and onto his stomach. Neither of us cares as we gaze at each other.

My pussy is aching and throbbing, and I know in that moment I'll never get enough of this man. Bryson's eyes are hooded, and his thick cock is still hard inside of me.

Something tells me neither of us is finished with each other yet.

13

TESSA

"Good Morning, Tessa," Bryson says, as I step into his office.

"Morning," I say, shrugging my jacket off and hanging it on the coat hook of his door. I can't meet his gaze. He hasn't mentioned our crazy sex-filled night of passion since.

Today is the *fourth* day since we started working together, and the fourth morning since I woke in his bed, his cum still dripping from my pussy. We'd fucked five times that night, and Bryson was like a wild animal. I came more times than I could even count. I'm not going to lie. I loved every single minute of it.

Ever since, it's all I can think about. To say it's awkward working together is an understatement. I keep catching him staring at me, or vice versa. All I want is to feel his cock stretch me again. Bryson has got under my skin so deep.

Not to mention, we've barely got anywhere with uncovering the perpetrator of the embezzlement scheme.

Bryson is typing on his computer. "Any news?" I ask. I left here late last night. It was about nine, but he said he was going to keep digging.

He shakes his head. "No, I still can't get to the bottom of this."

"How late were you here last night?"

He glances up at me and stretches his arms above his head. "I worked until eleven and then slept on the sofa." He nods toward the blanket on the sofa.

"Bryson, it's not good for you to work this hard," I say, stepping toward him. He has been working late for the past four nights.

I'm worried about him, which is ridiculous considering I didn't like the guy, but a night of the best sex I've ever had seems to change everything.

"I can't sit by and do nothing. If I don't sort this out and nip it in the bud, I'll lose my position as CEO to my brother."

He wants to be CEO. Even though, as we've been working together, it has become clear his brain is not geared up for finance. He doesn't get numbers the way I do. It's a little surprising for a man in charge of a financial company.

"Can you look at this for me?" he asks, pointing at his computer.

I draw in a deep breath and walk toward him, aware of the way he scans my body up and down, returning his eyes to my face. It makes me so hot that I'm not sure I can resist straddling him right here and now.

We've kept it professional since that night, to my disappointment, but he's not exactly subtle with his glances. I grab my reading glasses out of my pocket and put them on. Then I glance over his shoulder at the screen.

"Another expense sheet from the construction company?" I ask, shifting closer to the computer and grabbing the calculator from his desk.

"Yeah, I'm not the best with numbers, but I've got a feeling that this is worse than we thought." I can sense his eyes on me. Those beautiful, striking blue eyes that steal my breath from my lungs and make my pussy ache with need.

I type into the calculator, running the number through twice before taking a step back. *He's right.* The embezzlement total is closer to the tune of half a million dollars. The blood drains from my face. "Bryson, this is terrible," I say, swallowing hard.

He stands from his chair and grabs my hands in his. "Please don't tell me you're going to abandon me."

I swallow, enjoying his rough hands on me. My whole body heats, and I want him to fuck me right here. I pull my hands from his and shake my head. "Of course not. I told you I'm in, and I am, but this isn't good. Do you think we need to draw a line and call the feds in?"

The blood drains from his face. "We can't... I'd lose my position."

I draw in a deep breath, gazing into his eyes, which fill with panic. If there is one thing I've learned over these past four days, it's that Bryson is desperate to impress his father. It's kind of sweet that he cares so much. "We're talking about half a million dollars of money embezzled. Do you know how serious that is?"

He nods and rubs his face in his hands. His shoulders hunch over, and his whole demeanor seems defeated.

I run my hand along his muscular arm, trying not to think about how good he looked naked the other night. "You need to go home and get some sleep, Bryson."

He gazes up at me and shakes his head. "I'm not leaving this building until I've fixed this."

It has been becoming more and more difficult with each day I spend near Bryson to resist him. I thought maybe a passion-filled night would have quenched my desire for him. Instead, I want him more. My nights fill with ridiculous sexual fantasies about us, but it can't happen again. He's my boss. It was a onetime thing.

A cough startles us apart. Charlotte is standing in the doorway, holding some files in her hand. "I've got the documents you requested, sir," she says.

Bryson walks towards her and takes the file. "Thanks, Charlotte."

She smiles at him and bats her eyelashes in a way that makes a silly jealousy rise inside of me. I want everyone to know Bryson is mine, which is ridiculous. Bryson is my boss.

"Can I get you anything else, sir?"

"No, that is everything. Thank you, Charlotte."

She nods and shoots me a dirty look before walking away and shutting the door behind her.

I'd expected Bryson to flirt heavily with female staff, given the rumors I'd heard about him. Still, since we started working together, I'd barely seen him bat an eyelid at the beautiful women who come in here to bring him papers to sign or coffee. Perhaps that is all they were, rumors.

Deep down, I hope so. It's silly, but I want Bryson all to myself. We've fucked twice now, and he's all I want. He may be my boss, but my feelings towards him have only gotten stronger the more I get to know him. Something tells me the longer this goes on, the harder it will be to resist having sex with him again.

"Tessa, I wanted to go over these documents together." He holds up the file. "These are documents related to the construction company in question."

I nod and step back toward his desk, where he has pulled up another chair, which I sink into and cross one leg over my other. It's torture having to be so close to him all the time, and I'm not sure how long I'm going to be able to keep control of my urges.

Bryson's arm touches mine as he leans toward me and passes the paper into my hands, his fingers brushing against mine, sending lighting right to my core. Our eyes meet, and I see that hot, fierce look in his eyes that makes my thighs quiver. I glance down at the paper to break the tension, focusing on the words, despite the heat traveling through my body.

"What is it?" I ask, skimming through the wording.

Bryson leans over me and points to a clause in the paperwork. "From what I can tell, it's an order for the setup of the health and wellness account, and a man called Henry Rickshaw signed it." His brow furrows as he turns his attention to another document. "According to the records, he doesn't even exist. So, it's a dead-end, but someone must have signed this."

I sigh. "How are we supposed to find someone that doesn't exist?"

He gazes at me. "I don't know." His shoulders dip. "I was hoping you may have had an idea."

"I could try a background search for anyone with the same name," I suggest, shrugging. "I may be able to cross-reference it with anyone who lived in Wynton or who may have involvement."

Bryson smiles his heart-fluttering smile at me. "Perfect. I knew you'd have some idea what to do." The tension between us becomes palpable as we stare at each other for a few beats. Heat is burning through me like wildfire at being so close to this man. His face turns serious and shifts closer to me. I'm almost sure he's about to kiss me again, which I want more than anything. But, I resist.

I cough and avert my gaze to the file. "I'll do that now, sir," I say, reaching for the file, but he doesn't remove his hand.

"Tessa…" his voice is husky as he says my name. It sends a thrill through me. "Thank you," he says, clearing his throat and moving his hand.

I frown. "For what?"

He shakes his head. "For all of this, for being here and helping me out."

He is different from what I expected. After he was such an asshole to me on our telephone interview over two years ago when I applied, I assumed he was an arrogant prick. Perhaps he was having a bad day. "Your welcome," I say, grabbing the paper and moving away from him. Thankful to put some much-needed distance between us before I do something I regret—*again*.

14

BRYSON

The tapping of Tessa's fingers moving across the keyboard echoes through my office. I'm watching her from my desk, unable to think of anything else.

It's been two weeks since we fucked *five* times in one night. I've never wanted a woman the way I want her. Pure, primal, possessive feelings have been ruling me since the day we met. It's taking every ounce of restraint not to grab her and *take* her right here on my desk.

It has also been two weeks since we started investigating, and we've got no closer to finding the people involved in this. Whoever's behind this is smart, *very* smart. It's becoming difficult to concentrate around the beautiful accounting analyst who I keep catching staring at me.

I wonder if she wants to repeat that night again as *much* as I do.

"How are you getting on?" she asks, meeting my gaze.

My cock swells and thickens in my pants as she bites her bottom lip.

"The same old shit. Maybe we should grab some lunch and get out of here for an hour. It's no good being cooped up in this office for hours on end." I hook my finger under the knot of my tie and loosen it before unbuttoning the first few buttons on my shirt. When I glance up at Tessa, she is staring at me through hooded eyes, the desire unmissable.

"Is that a good idea?"

I can't understand why she would think having lunch is a bad idea unless she is referring to the last time we were in a restaurant together.

My brow raises. "We've got to eat, and taking breaks is important for both our health and sanity." I stand, grabbing my jacket off the back of my desk chair and shrugging it over my shoulders.

When I turn around, she is staring at me, as if she doesn't realize I'm waiting for her to get ready to leave. "We haven't got time to be taking breaks," she says, breaking eye contact and glancing down at her desk.

"Tessa." My voice has changed now from soft to commanding. "I will not ask you again. Get your jacket and let's *go.*" At the end of the day, I'm her boss, and I'm telling her we're going for lunch.

She trembles in her chair before standing and grabbing her jacket off the back of my office door. I'm already stepping toward her, closing the gap between us, as she shrugs her coat over her shoulder and then turns to me.

She jumps at how close I am, and her cheeks turn even redder. I smile at the effect I have on her. "Ready?"

She swallows hard. "M-My bag," she nods toward the handbag slung over the back of her chair.

I walk back to retrieve it, grabbing it and returning to her side. As I hand it to her, I brush my fingers against hers. Anytime I find a moment to get my skin touching hers, I do. All I want is to feel her curvy, hot body pressed against me *again*, totally fucking naked.

I'm a lover of torture, inviting this woman who drives me *wild* to join me for lunch. My cock is hard in my pants, as I follow her out into the corridor, watching her hips and ass sway as she walks in her mid-height heels. All I can picture is how good her ass looks naked.

She is right. This is a *bad* idea. I can't find it in me to give a shit. I've endured two weeks of *pure* torture around this woman and a shit load of hard work. We both deserve a short break, even if I can't stop thinking about fucking her *again*.

As we enter the elevator, I can't help myself and rest my hand on the small of Tessa's back. She freezes next to me and glances my way, but she doesn't say anything as another woman steps into the elevator with us. It moves downward, and I keep my hand on her back, resisting the urge to inch lower to her tight ass.

The elevator stops on the fourth floor, and the lady steps out.

Once the doors close, Tessa steps away from me and glares at me. "What are you doing?"

"Nothing, I only had my hand on your back."

She shakes her head. "Bryson, it's not professional for you to touch me in that *way*. You agreed that one night was a *onetime* thing."

I hold my hands up. "You're acting like I tried to stick my cock up your ass."

She turns even redder. "It's also not professional to speak to me like *that*." Her voice is small and fragile.

"Okay, sorry. I'll keep it professional," I say, as a *ding* rings out between us and the elevator doors open to the lobby.

She marches out and away from me, giving me a perfect view of that ass. I'm not sure she realizes what she does to me, but I need to keep control before I piss her off, and she decides this isn't worth the hassle anymore.

I follow her out into the fresh spring air and take in a deep breath. She's standing on the side, tapping her foot on the sidewalk.

"Tom is waiting for us over there," I say, pointing at the limo parked on the other side of the street.

She nods and heads across the street, not looking. My heart races as I rush into a sprint after her and grab her hand, pulling her back onto the pavement and out of the way of the bus *barreling* right toward her. She's in my arms in the nick of time as the bus charges past us.

Her eyes are wide, and her breathing is labored.

"Tessa, what the hell are you thinking?" I ask,

glancing down at her in shock. She almost *died* in front of my eyes, and I've *never* been so scared.

She shakes her head. "I-I wasn't."

Tom turns the limo around and pulls across the street, rolling the window down. "I'm sorry, sir. I tried to park closer, but there was no space when I arrived."

I nod. "Don't worry, Tom." I grab Tessa's shaking hand and help her into the limo.

She is in a state of shock and is silent for a good few minutes as the limo pulls away toward the diner. "You saved my life," she says, finally.

"Thank God. You were almost hit by a *bus*." My stomach is a mess of nerves as I stare at her. Without even thinking, I place my hand on her knee, as a comforting move rather than anything else.

Her eyes widen as she looks down, but she doesn't move away. Her whole body is shaking beneath my palm.

"Come here," I say, placing my arm around her shoulders, pulling her into my chest.

She sobs, clearly in shock. I'm still reeling from it. The moment I saw her stepping out and the bus *hurtling* toward her, it was as though time slowed down.

I hold her in my arms for the *entire* ride to the diner, feeling so protective of her. I want to wrap her up in cotton wool after what just happened. How could she be so careless?

She hasn't said another word as we pull up in front of the diner I often have lunch at.

"Are you okay?" I pull back to look into her tear-stained face.

She nods. "Yeah, it was such a shock. I still can't believe I almost got hit by a bus."

I wipe away her tears and grab her hand. "Come on. You need something to eat," I say, getting out of the limo and helping her out.

I don't let go of her hand, and she lets me hold it as we head into the dinner. Only once we are sat opposite each other, safely in the booth, do I let go.

She gives me a weak smile and gazes down at the menu in front of her.

I can't seem to bring myself to take my eyes off of her. It's as though I'm scared she'll disappear if I do. How can I keep going on like this when she is *all* I want? Usually, when I've had sex with a woman, she loses her appeal—not Tessa, though. I want her more than before.

"What are you going to have?" I ask, studying her.

She shrugs. "I've never been here before. What's good?"

"The bacon cheeseburger is good," I reply, smiling at her. It's crazy how happy I am when I'm around this woman.

"Then that's what I'll have, and a chocolate milkshake."

"Great choice, I'll have the same," I say, as I gesture for the waitress, Cindy. She takes our order, and a tense silence settles between us.

"Sir, can I ask you a question?"

"You did, but you can ask me anything."

She looks a little uncertain before opening her mouth. "Why do you want to be CEO of the company when you don't have an affinity with numbers?"

The question stings a little. Sure, I'm pretty shit at math, and that seems like an important skill for a CEO of a huge financial company, but I *love* to lead. "Running a company isn't *all* about the numbers. That's what the accounting staff are for." I run a hand through my hair. "I like to lead. It's what I'm good at," I say, trying not to let her read how much her question hurt me.

"Sorry, Bryson, it's just something that has been on my mind."

I nod and smile. "You've got nothing to be sorry about, Tessa. Why do I need to be good at numbers when I've got you by my side?"

She shrugs, reddening a little.

"Seriously, you're the most intelligent person I know, Tessa. I'm lucky to have you working for Stafford Financial."

I want to tell her I'm lucky to see her beautiful face every day. That I wish I woke up next to her lying beside me in my bed every single day, but I remember her warning about being professional and rein it in. The longer we spend time together, the harder it is to keep things professional.

15

TESSA

"At last, you're back," Bryson says, as I step into the office two minutes late from my break. I stepped out to grab a coffee as it was six o'clock in the evening.

I glance down at my watch to make sure I'm not that late. "Sir, I'm sorry I ran a few minutes behind."

He shakes his head. "I think I've found something significant."

My heart skips a beat. "Really?"

He nods and gestures for me to come over to his desk. I put my reading glasses on and read through an email between Mrs. Davis and a generic admin email address. It has some rather incriminating evidence that Mrs. Davis has something to do with this, although we still don't know who set it *all* up. No doubt, the person behind the admin address.

"Bryson, this is great."

It has been four weeks since we started investigating, and I was *almost* ready to throw in the towel and call the feds. The investigation into the embezzlement scheme is proving more difficult than either of us imagined, but this is the first step toward learning the truth.

Not to mention, it's been pure torture working with this man every day. All I can think about is how much I want him to fuck me again. Let's say, my dildo has been getting a lot of action in the past four weeks.

"Who do you think is behind this admin email address?" I ask.

Bryson sighs. "I tried to find out who set it up, but there are no logs on the address creation or which computer was used. At least we have one culprit tied to the scheme." He gazes into my eyes and steals the breath from my lungs for a moment, making me heat.

He can make my heart rate speed up with *one* look. All this time spent around him is making it far more difficult to control my urges.

Every night, he appears in my warped sex dreams after that night of passion and hotter sex than I've ever experienced. Ever since he saved my life, it has gotten worse.

He's always touching my arm or taking my hand in his, and it's getting more and more difficult not to jump him.

"I'll try to do more digging on this." I move away, breaking the tension. "I'm good with computers."

It's something I noticed with Bryson. He doesn't have

an affinity with computers or numbers. I wonder whether he enjoys working at the company. Surely, he would be better suited to something he naturally excels.

I sit back down at my desk and wake up my computer, but as I sit there, staring at Bryson, my mind wanders to our hot night in his apartment and our first fuck in the park. I never agree with public displays of affection, but I lost control. Sure, no one was around, but it was hot as hell.

The way his thick cock felt stretching me. The way he held me against the tree stump and fucked me until I came was amazing. I want to feel it all again, even though I know that can't happen. He's my boss. I need to restrain myself.

I glance over at him as he works hard at his desk, typing on his keyboard.

Bryson is nothing like I expected from all the rumors and stories. I was surprised to find how driven and hard-working he is. He is taking his acting CEO role seriously. He has been kind, funny, and generous, and I've thought about him as more than my boss, which is *very* bad.

Bryson glances at me and catches me staring right at him. "Any luck?"

Shit.

I glance at my blank computer screen and realize I've zoned out, thinking about him fucking me for far too long. I can feel my cheeks burning. "No, it's going to take a while," I say, averting his gaze and focusing on the document on my desk.

The creak of Bryson's leather office chair draws my attention back to him. He's leaning back in the chair with his eyes shut. His hands are behind the back of his neck. "Me neither. This is far harder than I believed it would be," he says.

My mouth dries as I let my eyes wander over him. His muscular body is straining against that tight shirt and his beautiful face. He's the most stunning man I've ever met, and I fucked him. His eyes shoot open, and he catches me *again*.

I shuffle under his gaze. "I know. It feels like we're never going to get to the bottom of this."

A panty-melting smile spreads across his lips. "We'll get there. We have to."

He is such an optimist, something that surprised me about him. He keeps surprising me. I can't stop my mind from running wild about this man, and it's not because he fucked me the way no other man has—I'm starting to like him as a person.

I know how dangerous it is to feel something for him. He would never be interested in me in that way. It was a hot office affair—a fling—nothing more.

I nod and return my attention to the document. I'm supposed to be digging into this and who was behind the email address, but I can't think of anything but Bryson.

"I'm getting a little tired." I glance at the clock to see it's almost seven-thirty at night. It's silent in the building.

He stands and walks toward me. "Yeah, maybe we should call it a night. Or…" He looks a little uncertain as he stares at me. "I could order dinner in for us if you would like?"

I run a hand through the loose waves of my hair and bite my bottom lip. Even though I'd love an excuse to spend more time with this man, I know it's a *bad* idea. My feelings toward him have been getting far too complicated. Not to mention, I can't trust my crazy hormones to behave. "I'm not sure that's a good idea."

His brow furrows. "I think eating is a good idea, considering how hard you've worked today." He sets his hand over mine. "You look a little pale. I don't want you fainting on me *again*."

I shake my head. "I'm not *even* hungry."

The last time we had dinner, I ended up straddling him in the limo and grinding against him, which lead to a passion-filled night of the *hottest* sex of my life.

"If you're sure, Tessa, I don't want you to feel I'm taking advantage of my position and not taking care of you as an employee." He runs a hand through his hair. "I know I've asked a lot from you these past four weeks. The most important thing is taking care of your health; eating is important."

Heat travels through me and settles in my cheeks. I'd like him to take care of me in a way that doesn't involve food. His huge, thick cock is stretching my pussy and making me come would be much more satisfying.

No, I can't be thinking like that.

Bryson Stafford is a billionaire and my boss. He would

never want a nerdy accounting analyst from the first floor.

There's one thing I'm sure of. That I won't rest until I've helped Bryson in any way possible to expose those involved and impress his father. It has become clear to me over the last four weeks that it's important to him. His father's opinion of him isn't great. It sounds like it more or less matched my opinion of him until I got to know him.

"What about this file? Did it reveal anything?" he points at another file I've barely delved into yet because of my crazy daydreams.

I shake my head. "No, there's nothing that gives away where the money has gone. It's as though it vanished."

Bryson steps closer, and my eyes travel to his crotch, which is bulging. It often is when we're close, and it's almost impossible to forget how *large* he is. The ache deep between my thighs makes my panties soak through. The fact is, I'm starving for this man, desperate for him.

His heady sandalwood scent fills the surrounding air, making my thighs clench.

A few times, I'd walked up to him and found his cock was hard, tenting his pants. The bulge makes me want to free it from his pants and impale myself on him.

"Are you sure I can't order some food in?"

I want to say *yes*, but I can't. Bryson is my boss, and this is *too* complicated. Dinner could lead to more hot sex if I don't get the hell away from him.

16

BRYSON

I stand over her, waiting for her reply. My cock is as hard as a stone. I've proposed we have dinner together, and she is rejecting me. It makes me crazy.

I need her to agree, even though I know how dangerous it is, considering the only thing I want to feast on right now is Tessa.

"Thank you for your concern, but I think we should get some rest. We've been working hard non-stop for the past four weeks."

I feel irritated by her second refusal. "Okay, let's finish up then." I turn and sit back down at my desk to shut down my desktop.

I find my gaze returning to her. Even though she says she is tired, she looks as *sexy* as ever. The more I get to know her, the more difficult it becomes to keep my mind out of the gutter.

I swallow hard as my eyes travel to her full cleavage, and the memory of her full, perky breasts bouncing while she sucked my cock flash into my mind. Tessa never looks tired. Her brain and drive are impressive. I'm not sure how she gets the willpower to work with numbers *all* day. They give me a damn headache.

She's helped me, though. Over the past four weeks, she's taught me things I never thought I'd grasp. I've been enamored with her ever since we met. She begs me to fuck her against that tree in the park.

But as I've got to know her, I've started to feel more than desire or sexual attraction. The way she laughs is beautiful, her mind is sexy as hell, and she's the most interesting woman I've ever met.

She lets out a long sigh before stretching her arms over her head. I admire her curvy body. I've masturbated in the last four weeks more than I ever have, even more than when I was a teenager. I've had to slip into the bathroom and relieve myself more times than I can count, and every single time, I remember the way she felt as I sunk my cock deep inside of her.

I watch her stand and focus on her hips swaying as she walks toward the erase board set up in my office. Her tight *ass* looks fucking amazing in the skirt she's wearing today. She wipes everything off the board. It's her customary routine at the end of all our sessions. We can't leave any evidence of what we're investigating.

For the first time in my life, I find myself drawn to an intelligent woman. In the past, it's been easier to stick to the leggy models who know nothing about finance. I think I've always been too scared to open myself up to scrutiny. I'm the acting CEO of a thriving financial company, and I can't stand working with numbers. It's ridiculous. My weakness in finance makes me vulnerable. Tessa already knows my weakness, and I don't mind her knowing.

Her jasmine scent infuses everything in my office, and it drives me *wild*. I can't tear my eyes away from her as she turns to gather up the papers and documents on my desk. Her eyes meet mine, and my cock jumps in my pants.

She stands upright *too* quickly, sensing the sexual tension charging the air. We both know that we can't cross that line *again*. The only one that doesn't know it in this room is my rock-hard dick.

She steps away and goes to remove a pen she used to hold her hair up in a messy bun. I watch as she tries to pull out the pen and free her flowing wavy hair. The pen snags and gets stuck.

She turns away, her cheeks reddening as she fights to remove it. I stand, intending to help her. My mind screams, it's a bad idea, but I can't stop myself. My hands settle on her hips, and I pull her close. "Tessa…" I say softly, making her tense. "Let me help you with that."

Her hands drop to the side as mine tangle in her hair. My cock leaks precum into my boxer briefs as memories of our wild night heat me like nothing else *ever* has.

I free her pen from her hair and pass it into her

hands, lingering a moment as my finger brushes her soft skin. A visible shiver passes through her. "Thank you, Bryson." Her voice is quiet, but I *love* hearing my name from her lips.

I need to move away from her, but my cock seems to have taken control of my brain. It was supposed to be only one night, but *fuck* it. The sudden need to press her tight body to mine overwhelms me, and I tighten my grip on her waist and pull her back into my chest. My hard cock presses against her ass.

"Bryson..." she gasps, arching her back.

I move her flowing hair out of the way and kiss her neck, making her *moan* as my lips touch the sensitive skin.

I *groan* against her skin.

I need to be inside this woman *again*, right here and right now. I lose control and kiss every inch of exposed skin on her shoulder and neck before spinning her around and claiming her lips. I'm lost, lost in this woman that drives me wild with need.

She cups my hard, throbbing cock through my pants, her dainty fingers gripping hold and stroking me through the fabric.

"Tessa..." I groan her name, making her moan as I deepen the kiss, thrusting my tongue into her mouth.

She wants this as much as I *need* this. Finally, I feel sane again with her against me after four weeks of resisting these *crazy* urges to make her mine.

My arm tightens around her waist, and I pick her up, carrying her toward my desk.

"I can't resist you anymore, Tessa. It is torture," I say, setting her down on the edge of my desk and pushing her skirt up to her hips, exposing her wet panties.

She moans and kisses me hard. "I can't stop thinking about that night at your apartment."

I growl and kiss her with even more desperation. She feels the same, but the question is, does she want me the way I want her?

Forever.

My finger slides up her thigh, teasing her and making her quiver. Her lacy panties are soaked through as I reach the fabric and run a finger from her clit, right down her slit and back up.

She shudders beneath me and throws her head back. Her eyes shut tight, and her cheeks are flushed. She looks even better than I remember in my apartment or against that tree.

I hook my finger into the waistband of her panties and pull them down over her thighs, exposing her swollen, glistening pussy to me. She's soaking. "Fuck, Tessa, you're so wet for me."

I kiss a path up her thighs, slowly trailing kisses higher and higher until I reach her dripping arousal, making her moan.

"Do you want to feel my lips on your pussy again, baby?"

She nods, biting her bottom lip gently. I taste her slit first with a light flick of my tongue. Her sweet nectar is even *better* than I remember. I rest my hand flat on her stomach, holding her down as she bucks her hips in desperation.

I forget where I am or what I'm doing. All that matters right *now* is Tessa. She becomes my world, and I have to drink every drop of her. It is like I'm addicted to her.

She squirms beneath me as I feast on her pussy, enticing the sweetest sounds from her lips. My finger slides between her soaking wet folds, before plunging inside of her and driving deep. I curl my finger, finding the perfect spot inside her that makes her shake.

"Bryson," she moans my name and then tangles her fingers in my hair. I run my teeth over her clit, and she bucks into me again. "Fuck, Bryson, please…"

I pull back to gaze into her beautiful face. "What do you want, baby?" I ask, staring up into those emerald eyes dilated with longing.

"You," she rasps out.

"Tell me what you want. I want to hear you say it," I growl.

Her cheeks redden, and she bites her lip in a way that makes me want to lose control. "I want you to *fuck* me."

I can't stifle the groan in my chest as my cock gets harder. It feels like it might burst from my pants. I bring my lips to Tessa's, kissing her and making her taste her sweet juices. "I'm going to make you come first, but only when your boss says you can. Do you understand me?" I whisper into her ear.

She nods. "Yes, sir."

I return to working her into a frenzy. I lick and nip at her sensitive, swollen clit, driving two fingers in and out of her tight pussy.

"This feels as good as I remember," I growl, curling my fingers inside her.

Her emerald eyes dilate with lust as she watches me suck her clit into my mouth and finger fuck her pussy, making her moan.

Tessa shudders and bucks against my hand, forcing me deeper. She's moaning the sweetest noises I've ever heard, as I fuck her with my fingers. I add a *third* finger inside of her.

Her tight pussy clenches around me as I lick and suck at her clit. The muscles flutter around my fingers, warning me she is getting closer to exploding. "Please, Bryson, I can't…"

She shudders as I tighten my grip around her legs and push her further, revealing her perfect asshole to my view. I trace it with my finger, sending tremors through her body. My tongue teases at her asshole, pushing further inside of her forbidden hole.

She gasps as I tease her there, making her whole body tense more. "Oh my God," she moans.

Her pussy is dripping as I lick and tongue fuck her ass, making her more and more crazy. Her body winds so tightly as I run the tip of my tongue through her soaking wet lips, tasting her more deeply.

The muscles flutter around my tongue, warning me she isn't going to last much longer. I told her to wait for my permission to come, and she's holding on like a good girl.

Her fingers tighten in my hair, and she begs me. "Please, Bryson... I need to come..." she cries out.

"Then come for me, come all over my fingers, and let me lick every drop of your sweet cum from you," I growl.

Her body trembles as she screams, "Fuck, *Bryson*." The muscles around my fingers tighten as she comes on my desk. I withdraw my fingers, lapping up every drop of the sweet juice spilling from her. I suck on her lips, tasting all of it. I can't get enough.

Luckily, it's past eight o'clock at night. No one else is here because otherwise, everyone would know what we were doing in my office. She's panting on my desk as her pussy drips onto my tongue.

I lick her one more time before returning my lips to her mouth. I kiss her hard, letting her taste herself on my tongue.

Her hands move for my buttons, undoing my shirt and pushing it off. She pulls me to her again, kissing my chest, and her hands worship my rippled abs. I enjoy the feel of her soft skin all over my body.

I move my hands to her blouse and undo it. I need to see her perfect, plump breasts on display and suck her hard nipples into my mouth. This woman is my obsession.

She helps me remove her blouse, shrugging it from her shoulders. Then I unhook her bra, freeing her breasts, and groan as her nipples are peaked toward me, so hard. They are the perfect breasts.

I pinch each one between my finger and thumb, before circling each pebbled nipple with my tongue and then sucking on them, making her *gasp*.

Her hands go to my belt, and she releases it. She pulls my pants down to expose my *bulging* boxer briefs. She drops to her knees in front of me and frees my hard cock, gripping the base in her hands.

It always looks even *bigger* with her small fingers wrapped around the thick base, and her lips only inches from the tip. My cock twitches in her hand, and her tongue darts out to lick the liquid from the tip.

I *groan*, squeezing my eyes shut. Tessa's lips feel perfect around my thick shaft as her tongue swirls around the swollen head of my cock. I buck my hips forward, driving myself deeper into her throat. She moans as she takes more of me inside her mouth.

I open my eyes and watch as she swallows my cock. Her emerald eyes gaze up at me, dilated with longing. My balls ache, and my cock throbs in her mouth, making me harder.

Her beautiful breasts bounce around as she bobs her head up and down my cock. "Tessa, your mouth feels fucking perfect." I grip her hair in my fist.

My cock leaks thick precum down her hot throat. It feels so fucking good. If I let her suck me much longer, I'm going to cum down her throat. I grip her wrist, forcing her to stop sucking and gaze up at me.

"Bend over my desk, baby," I command.

She stands, and I watch her tight ass and hips sway as she walks, naked, toward my desk. She gazes over her shoulder as she bends right over, giving me a perfect view of that beautiful pussy and her tight little asshole. I fist my cock in my hand for a moment, memorizing this image of her.

"Are you going to fuck me, sir?" she asks.

Sir.

I love the way it sounds when she calls me, sir. I move toward her swollen pussy and rub the head of my cock through her dripping wet folds. "Are you ready for my cock?" I growl.

She whimpers in response, arching her back to push back on me. I grab hold of her hips, pulling her toward me.

"Do you want to feel your boss's cock stretching you?" I ask again.

She nods her head and gazes back at me. "Yes, sir, *please.*"

That's *all* it takes. I thrust myself deep inside Tessa's tight, wet arousal. She squeezes around me, tightening around my thick shaft. It takes me a moment to get used to the way she feels. There's no going back *now*.

I'm going to *claim* my employee on top of my desk, and I no longer give a shit. Tessa is *mine*.

17

TESSA

*B*ryson's slaps my ass, making me groan. The sound of his hand slapping my skin echoes around the cavernous office. I moan and buck my hips as he moves his huge cock in and out of me. I *love* being at the mercy of this man.

It's the first time since we fucked four weeks ago that I feel satisfied. Bryson speaks to me in such a filthy way, and I've never been so turned on.

Bryson Stafford is a sex god—a beautiful, muscular sex god. The way he makes me come is better every single time. I'm not sure how it is possible, but I'm so desperate for this man, and it's only growing the longer I know him.

Our heavy breathing fills the air as he moves in and out of me, making me tense around him. I want him to fuck me hard and take me for all I'm worth.

Bryson holds still inside of me for a moment, making

me whimper. I try to buck my hips, and he tightens his grip on my hips, holding me in place. "I'm in charge, Tessa." The way he says my name spreads liquid fire through my belly. "Do as your boss commands," he growls.

"Yes, sir," I moan.

He licks a path up the column of my neck and then thrusts into me hard and deep, lighting up every sensitive nerve inside me. He stops again, holding still inside of me with maddening restraint. It doesn't matter how badly I need to feel him fucking me hard and fast. He's teasing me.

My body is wound tightly and ready. Before I met Bryson, I'd never considered having sex in a public place. Since meeting him, we've fucked in a park and now in his office. It's as if I'd do anything for him.

He grips my throat and forces my back to arch toward him. "Tell me how much you want me to *fuck* you, Tessa."

My pussy gushes at the command in his voice. I never expected to love a man being so forceful with me during sex. "I want you to fuck me more than anything I've ever wanted."

His grip tightens around my throat. "Tell me how you want it, baby."

"I want it hard and fast," I rasp out.

He growls and then pulls his huge cock out, so his throbbing head is still inside of me, and then drives right back into me. I *scream* in pure ecstasy as he does it over and over again. I feel my body quiver with unadulterated pleasure as he fucks me *harder* than I've ever been fucked in my life.

"Fuck, Bryson," I *scream* his name as he edges me closer and closer to my second orgasm. The way he fucks me is rough and dominating, and I love every second of it.

"Scream my name." He slaps my ass as he pumps into me again. A stinging pain that turns into throbbing pleasure, adding to the sensation of his cock taking me hard and fast. I'm teetering on the edge of explosion as he pulls back out of me and plunges inside of me hard and fast. His hand comes down on my other ass cheek, and it tips me over the edge of the cliff.

"Bryson, I'm coming, *Bryson*," I scream, as my muscles clamp around his thick cock so hard it feels like I'm trying to keep him there forever, but he keeps pumping into me even harder and faster. He fucks me through my orgasm, heightening every sensation.

I'm not even sure what sounds I'm making. My vision begins to blur, and he keeps fucking me.

"That's it, baby, come on your boss's cock," He growls as he lets go of my neck, and I flop back down onto his desk.

He doesn't stop, though. He pumps in and out of me more slowly as my body comes down from the most explosive orgasm I've ever experienced. My body relaxes around him, but he's still pumping in and out of me. "Turn around," he orders.

He pulls out, to my dismay. If I had my way, his cock

would stay inside of me permanently. I stand on my shaking legs and turn.

His muscular arms lock around me, and he lifts me to my feet. "How flexible are you?"

My brow furrows. "I can do the splits."

His eyes light up as he grabs my arms and forces me to lock them around his neck, hooking one arm under my knee and lifting my leg. My soaking wet pussy is open to him while I stand on one shaky limb. He bends his knees, and his hard cock slides into me.

I gasp as he captures my lips with his. He pulls back and growls, "You may like it hard and fast, but it's my turn to give it to you how I *want*."

He pulls back and gazes into my eyes as he pumps in and out of me, driving inside me deeper than ever before. Each thrust hits the perfect spot inside of me. A shiver runs from the top of my head and down my spine. I'm not even sure if I've come down from my orgasm yet as he begins to build the pressure once again.

My mind is blank. I can barely think straight as he keeps his hand tight around my leg, keeping it elevated to make it easier to drive deep into me. The wet sounds of our bodies meeting and heavy breathing fill the room. His dick is so long and thick, stretching me perfectly.

Somehow, this is hotter than the night in his apartment, as he kisses me passionately, stealing the breath from my lungs. The intensity increases as we fuck, staring into each other's eyes. I'm making noises that I've *never* made before.

His grunts are animalistic, and he looks like he is *lost*. This is the most passionate sex I've ever experienced, even more passionate than the first time. I can feel the pressure building deep within me again with every thrust. The eye contact between us becomes almost too much, and I shut my eyes and let my head rollback.

Bryson's hand circles my throat, making me even wetter. "Look at me, Tessa," he commands.

I feel the pressure deep inside of me, building to new levels. His deep voice only adds to the thrilling pleasure running through me. I force myself to open my eyes, gazing into his. I need to release it again. Sex has *never* been this good before.

"I want to gaze into your eyes as I fuck you. I want to look into your eyes as you come on my cock *again*." He captures my lips, and I know I'm about to come.

The rhythm becomes more frantic as my pussy tightens around him. He pulls away from my lips and gazes deep into my eyes. Bryson grunts with every thrust, as if he's struggling to hold on to his control. He's waiting until I come again. He bites my lip gently and then sucks on it, making me moan and whimper.

I can feel my orgasm rushing toward me at a hundred miles an hour, as an even more explosive orgasm rocks through me, making my vision white around the edges. My mouth falls open, and I think I make a sound, but I can't be sure.

It's the most intimate experience I've ever had. Stars dance in my vision as Bryson holds my gaze. I come around his cock, muscles tightening hard around him. My body feels used and spent as spasm after spasm coils through my muscles. If it weren't for Bryson's strong arms holding me up, I'd collapse on the floor.

He *grunts* as he comes as well, gazing into my eyes as he unleashes his cum deep inside of me.

Heavy exhaustion spreads through my body, forcing me to clutch onto him for support. My knees shake beneath me.

As the after-effects of three consecutive and *explosive* orgasms wear off, they stop shaking. I claw on to Bryson's thick muscular arms and breathing heavily. I should regret fucking him again. We both vowed the night I went to his apartment was a *onetime* thing.

Four weeks later, neither of us could resist. The question is, what happens now? He's my boss. We can't keep fucking, no matter how much I want to.

I want to be with this man for *real*, and it scares me. He isn't going to want me like that.

18

BRYSON

I move away from Tessa in search of a towel for her to clean up. My gym towels are neatly folded in the dresser in the corner of my office.

A palpable silence has settled between us ever since we finished fucking. Does she regret having sex with me?

In the past, after I have sex with a woman, I don't have the unbelievable urge to do it again. Even four weeks couldn't tame the crazy, animalistic need to be with her. Once we submitted to our desire, we turned into wild animals, unable to get enough of each other. The crazy thing is, I want to fuck her repeatedly. It was as passionate as before, but even more intimate.

I return to her and hand her the towel. She smiles that beautiful, heart-wrenching smile, and I can feel my stomach twist with nerves.

What the fuck?

I'm never nervous around women.

"Thank you, Bryson," she says.

I watch her as she cleans herself up. My cock is stirring already at the sight of her naked in my office. She turns to grab her clothes off the floor, but I'm in front of her before she can grab them. I grip hold of her wrist and pull her toward me, kissing her soft lips.

I grab hold of her hips and then circle my arms around her waist, lifting and carrying her toward the large corner sofa in my office. "I want you to stay here for a bit with me," I say softly, settling on the sofa and pulling her into my arms.

We're both still naked. My cock is semi-hard again. She allows me to hold her in my arms and gazes up into my eyes. "We shouldn't have done that."

I chuckle. "We should have. I've been going mad these past four weeks. All I've been thinking about is fucking you again, baby." I kiss her lips quickly. "You're *mine*."

She tenses in my arms. Does she only see this as sex? Don't I only see this as sex?

No.

It has become clear during the past four weeks that this isn't *only* sexual attraction. Tessa is different from any woman I've ever known. She challenges me and pushes me to improve—she makes me want to be better.

"Come on. I'm going to take you for dinner," I say, shifting to move from the sofa.

Her eyes widen as she stares at me like I've gone mad.

"It's only polite, and you need to eat, Tessa."

I care about this woman. I never do normally, but it seems Tessa is the exception to *all* my rules.

"I-I don't think that's a good idea," she says.

I can't help but laugh. "You'll fuck me, but you'll draw the line at having dinner with me?" I raise an eyebrow.

She chuckles. "Fair enough. I'll get dressed." She shifts in an attempt to stand.

"Not so quickly," I say, tightening my grip on her and pulling her lips to mine. The kiss is soft at first, but before I know it, her hands tangle in my hair, and she's moaning against my mouth.

"Bryson..." She straddles me and grinds her soaking wet pussy against me, making me steel again.

"If you do that, then we'll never make it to dinner," I say. My cock is hard, straining against her pussy.

"Order in," she pleads, grinding against my cock.

She's so desperate for me, and it *drives* me wild. This woman wants me as badly as I want her. I'm not about to deny her.

"Okay," I whisper into her ear, nipping it in a way I know she loves as she arches her back and moans. "What do you want?"

"You," she rasps.

I chuckle. "I mean to eat."

She's still grinding against my cock, driving me mad.

"Pizza," she says.

"Okay, you're going to have to stop grinding on me while I make the call," I say.

She shifts from my lap. I go to grab my cell off my

desk, typing in a local delivery place number, knowing it will take a while. "Hello, I'd like to order—"

I glance down to find Tessa on her knees with my cock in her mouth. She's insatiable.

"Sir, hello, are you there?" the pizza guy asks.

Shit.

"Yes, sorry, can I get two medium pizzas? One pepperoni and the other..." I hold my hand over the receiver. "Tessa, what pizza do you want?"

She pulls her plump lips off of my hard cock. "Chicken and bacon, please," she says, before clamping her lips around my shaft and taking me deep into her throat.

"And one chicken and bacon," I say to the guy.

"Is that all, sir?"

"Yeah, that's all, delivery to The Stafford Financial Group building on 5th Avenue. Please leave it with the front desk." I hang up the phone after he has agreed, telling me it will be a half-hour wait.

Tessa is working my cock with her mouth, making me groan the moment I'm off the phone. I grab hold of her wrist, forcing her to her feet. "Tessa, you're a very bad girl, and I think I need to *punish* you."

Her eyes light up, and I know she likes being dominated. "On your knees with your beautiful fucking ass toward me," I command.

She does as I say, dropping to her knees. Her pussy is dripping with my thick cum, and her perfect asshole looks so inviting. I drop onto my knees behind her and lick her from her bottom right down to her clit. She makes the *sweetest* noise ever as I tease her tight little hole with my tongue and plunge my fingers into her wet pussy. I want to claim all her holes, but not right now.

She loves it when I lick her ass as she writhes beneath me, reacting to my tongue. I lick the tight little ring of muscle, making her wetter as I plunge three fingers in and out of her pussy.

It doesn't take long before she's shuddering beneath me, making my cock harder as her muscles spasm around my fingers.

"Bryson, please…" she gasps.

"What is it? You're a naughty girl who doesn't deserve to come," I say, slapping her ass.

She glances back at me, biting her lip. Her cheeks are flushed red, and she looks amazing—on her knees, open to me. I thrust my fingers in and out of her, making her moan louder and louder, taking her higher.

"Come on your boss's fingers," I say, slapping her ass again.

She screams as an orgasm rips through her, and her muscles tighten around my fingers *so* hard it almost hurts. Once she has finished, she collapses on the office floor spent.

"Turn around," I command. "On your knees."

She does as I say, playing with her hard nipples as she gazes at me.

"Open your mouth," I say.

She opens her mouth, and I slip my fingers in, forcing

her to taste herself. She licks and sucks at my fingers, cleaning them. "Do you like tasting yourself?" I ask.

She nods. "Please, Bryson…" Her eyes are pleading me.

"You're a bad girl who needs to be taught a lesson by her boss, aren't you?" I ask, knowing what she wants. My thick cock is stretching her tight pussy *again*. "On your hands and knees," I command, stroking my length.

She turns and bares herself to me, rolling her hips back. I can't hold off any longer as my cock twitches and spills precum onto the floor of my office. I grab hold of the base of my throbbing shaft and guide it to her soaking wet folds, rubbing the head in her slippery juices.

She's so wet for me.

I thrust into her, making her moan and buck back onto my cock, forcing me deep. My fingers dig into her hips as I move inside her again, pulling my cock almost all the way out and then driving back into her hard. The creamy skin of her ass is tinged pink from where I slapped her earlier, and I do it again, making her scream my name.

"Bryson… Fuck *me.*"

I get lost in her, hearing her beg me to fuck her snaps all my control. A *primal* and animalistic need to claim this woman drives me as I fuck her hard and deep, hitting that spot that makes her *scream* in pleasure with every thrust. It's as though we're the only two people that exist in the world at that moment.

The fluttering in her muscles hints she's ready to

come *again*, clamped hard around my aching cock. My heavy balls slap against her clit, making her moan with each thrust. My balls are aching for release, even though I came only forty minutes ago deep inside of her.

I circle my fingers around her throat, forcing her back to arch. I nip her ear lobe with my teeth. "You want to come on your boss's cock like a filthy little girl, don't you?" I growl, thrusting in hard. "You want to feel every drop of my cum spilling deep inside of you as I fill you up?"

Her eyes roll back in her head as I lick her neck and then bite it, leaving a mark. "Fuck... Yes, please," she rasps words out as I drive in deeper inside of her — the slap of skin against skin echoing around my cavernous office.

"Come for me, Tessa," I groan, driving into her even harder and faster now.

"*Bryson*," she screams my name, coming so hard around my cock.

I growl against the soft creamy skin of her neck as she forces me to come with her, dragging me right off the edge. Thick shots of hot cum release deep inside of her, making sure she's well and truly filled with my seed. Tessa is mine, and I'm making my mark on her.

We breathe heavily in silence for a long while. I try to get a grip of my senses, which I'd lost for a moment, fucking my employee.

Almost like clockwork, my desk phone rings a

moment later, forcing me to pull my cock from her and walk toward my desk, grabbing the phone. "Hello."

"Sir, there's a pizza delivery here for you," the receptionist says.

"Thank you. Can you send it up with the guard in the elevator please?" I ask.

Tessa's eyes widen, and she jumps to her feet, rushing around, grabbing her clothes and underwear from the floor. I smile at how adorable she is.

When I put the phone back down on the receiver, she spins toward me. Her eyes are wide. "It probably reeks of sex in here."

I laugh and shrug my shirt on, doing it up. Then grab my pants from the floor, putting them on and leaving my boxers and my belt off. As something tells me, we'll be naked again before we leave tonight if that night at my apartment is anything to go on. "Don't worry. I'll meet him at the elevator," I say, heading for the door.

The guard is up with the pizza a minute after I leave the room. I thank him and head back to Tessa—my Tessa. Her cheeks are pink and flushed, and she looks well fucked and more beautiful than ever.

"Come on, let's eat," I say, walking toward the sofa.

She's a little unsure at first, which is ridiculous. I just had my cock inside her for the second time tonight. She walks over and plops down on the sofa, grabbing her pizza.

We eat in comfortable silence, other than a few noises of satisfaction she makes. Once she's done, she closes the box and sets it on the coffee table. "That was damn good."

I raise an eyebrow. "My cock or the pizza?"

She bites her bottom lip. "Both."

"Tell me, Tessa, what made you want to be an accounting analyst?" I ask, wanting to know more about the woman who makes me lose control.

She sucks in her cheeks as if considering the question. "I love numbers. They're logical and can't lie to you," she says, the hint of hurt in her voice.

"Have people lied to you in the past?" I ask.

Her eyes seem to glaze over, and she nods, biting her lip. "Yeah, I've not had much luck in the relationship department."

I sigh. "Neither have I."

Her eyes narrow. "I heard you were a *playboy*."

I frown at her, wondering where she heard that. "I used to party a lot, but I wouldn't have classed myself as a playboy." I shake my head. "I've slept with a lot of women in my past, Tessa, but had no luck when it comes to love, and not for the lack of trying."

My heart was badly broken by Ella, my first girlfriend, when she ran off with my best friend from college. I haven't found a woman I could see myself being with since.

Tessa changes that. I can see myself with her forever. The question is, would she ever want to be with me for real?

19

TESSA

I wake the next morning with a sweet ache between my thighs, lying in my bed, wishing Bryson was next to me.

Bryson and I shared a wild and passion-filled night, and I didn't leave until almost one in the morning. Bryson insisted on escorting me home, but I didn't invite him in.

The night we met at the bar, we made a passion-filled mistake, not realizing that he was my boss. The next evening after dinner was foolish, but both of us needed each other.

Last night can't be a mistake. You can't make a mistake three times. It's more of an addiction. I'm addicted to my boss and the way he makes me feel. We'd had another night of mind-blowing sex that neither of us could resist.

My feelings toward Bryson aren't sexual. I think I've

known that since we met at the bar. We clicked in a way I've never clicked with anyone.

Bryson is hard to read. The worst thing is we ended up sitting together, chatting for hours. It felt natural, and I could feel myself getting more attached to him than I already was.

I press my wrist against my forehead and let out a long sigh. I've fallen for my boss.

Who the hell wouldn't?

The man is kind, caring, and makes my body react like it never has before. The sex is out of this world, but I've fallen for him in other ways since we started working together.

It's ridiculous, but it's true. Last night wasn't about sex for me, although I know it was for him. Why would Bryson Stafford want a nobody like me? He's a billionaire. He can have any sexy, beautiful model he desires. My chest aches at the thought.

I force myself out of bed and hurry to get ready. If I don't get a move on, I'm going to be late. Somehow, I'm going to work with Bryson today without letting last night's session get in the way. He made me come so many times. I couldn't count.

When I was with Ted, I was lucky if I came once anytime we had sex. I'd often finish myself off once he disappeared into the bathroom to clean up.

I dress for work and leave the apartment in record time. Despite the utter embarrassment I feel about even facing Bryson again, I can't let him down. Not after everything we've been through. We're so close to cracking this scheme and getting to the bottom of it. Once that it's dealt with, I can go back to normal, sitting in my office and forget that Bryson even exists.

Why does that thought make my chest ache?

I can't want Bryson. We're worlds apart — two different people. I head out of the apartment in a daydream, heading straight for work on auto-pilot. Before I know it, I'm staring up at the looming Stafford building. Dread blooms in my stomach.

How is Bryson going to act after last night? The last thing he should do when trying to impress his father is fucking one of his employees. It doesn't take a genius to figure that out.

After a few moments of hesitation, I step into the calming entrance of my work building. I sign myself in as normal before heading for the elevator. No one seems to have noticed how much time I've spent on the top floor, or even asked what I was doing there for the last four weeks. It's strange. Mrs. Davis doesn't even notice I'm not in my office.

The elevator ride goes on *forever*. I'm glad. I'm so anxious I'm not sure I even want to see Bryson again after last night. Nausea floods my gut as the elevator dings, signaling my arrival on the top floor. I step out and barrel straight into a handsome, tall, dark-haired man I've never seen before.

"Oh, sorry! I didn't see you there," I say.

He smiles down at me. His blue eyes are so similar to Bryson's. "No problem, Miss?" He gazes at me.

"Clayton, Tessa Clayton."

He smiles at me. "Theo Stafford." He holds out a hand for me to shake.

I shake it and then shuffle on the spot. "It's nice to meet you. I'm sorry I barged into you, sir." I bow my head, well aware that this is Bryson's brother.

"No problem. May I ask why you are up here?" His eyes narrow.

Heat travels through my body, straight to my cheeks. "I've got some files for Bryson Stafford. I'm on my way to his office now."

Theo cocks his head. "Files, huh? I hope he's not taking advantage of his position here at The Stafford Financial Group." He raises an eyebrow.

"Sorry, what are you insinuating?"

He shakes his head. "Nothing, Miss Clayton. Now, if you'd excuse me, I'm late for a meeting." He slips into the elevator and gives me a wink as the door shuts behind him.

My whole body is on fire. It's as if he knew I'd slept with Bryson. Is his brother renowned for sleeping with his employees? My heart sinks in my chest at the thought. I head toward Bryson's office and don't even think twice about letting myself in.

My mouth drops open as I walk in on Charlotte, his secretary, launching herself into his arms. I walk in to see her lips clash with his, and my heart breaks a little. The door slams shut behind me, bringing Bryson's attention to me. No doubt, my face is a picture of how I feel, and I can't even bring myself to speak with him right now. I turn and rush out the door.

"Tessa, *wait,*" he shouts after me.

I don't wait. I can't. How stupid to let myself fall for a man like him. He's no better than Ted. The elevator is waiting, and I jump straight in. I can hear Bryson's heavy footsteps barreling toward the elevator.

"Tessa, *stop.*"

I press the button to shut the door, and in the nick of time, the elevator shuts in his face and moves downward to the first floor. Tears prickle my eyes, but I don't allow them to fall. I hold them in. Intent on making it to my office before I let a single tear shed.

I'm thankful when the doors open to the first floor. I make my way toward my office, and once there, I let myself in and lock the door. Alone and away from anyone, the tears fall down my cheeks. I let Bryson Stafford in, and he broke my heart in record time. We slept together last night, and I walk in to find him kissing his secretary the next morning. He is the *worst* kind of man. I should have believed the rumors about him.

Heavy footsteps echo down the hallway toward my office, and my heart skips a beat. Surely, he hasn't come down to the first floor after me. The doorknob twists, but I locked the door. Three hard knocks follow.

I wipe my face with my hand. "Who is it?"

"Tessa, it's Bryson. Please let me in, so I can explain."

No way, I'm not letting him in, not after what I saw. "I'm sorry. I've got a conference call."

Bryson punches the door, sending a loud tremor through the room. "God damn it, Tessa. Let me in now before I break down this damn door down." His voice is desperate and angry.

I can't stand facing him, but I also can't deny the CEO of the company I work for. With a heavy heart, I stand and unlock the door. I then sit back behind my desk and focus on my computer. He opens the door and slips inside, but I can't even look at him.

"Tessa, what you saw isn't what you think," he starts.

I keep my eyes on my computer and read a couple of emails.

"Damn it, Tessa. Look at *me*."

I glance up at him because of the tone of his voice. "What do you want, sir?"

He clenches his jaw. "I didn't kiss Charlotte. She came on to me and launched herself at me. If you had waited a moment, you would have seen me fire her ass for it."

I raise an eyebrow. "That's an unlikely story. It's my fault for sleeping with you, since your reputation is well known. I should have known you sleep with many of your employees." I shake my head. "I should have known what you were like when you fucked me against the tree in the park."

Bryson slams his hand down on my desk, making me jump. "God damn it, Tessa. You've got no idea what you're talking about, no fucking idea." He runs a hand through his hair. "I've *never* slept with any employee at The Stafford Financial Group until you. Sure, I was a lothario when I was younger, but never here at work. You're the *only* one."

I shake my head, disbelieving his words. "That's bullshit."

"It's not bullshit, Tessa. It's the God damn truth." He glares into my eyes for a few moments, making heat travel across my skin as memories of the night before flood my mind. Before I can process what he is doing, he lifts me from my chair into his arms and kisses me hard.

I try to push him away. "What the fuck are you doing?" I shake my head. "I've been hurt by assholes like you before, and I'm not making the same mistake *again*."

"I'm not going to hurt you, Tessa. I want *you*. You and only you," he growls, capturing my lips again.

I relax into the kiss, unable to deny how good his lips feel against mine. The way he makes me feel is *addictive*. I wish his words were true, but this man is a player. A man that enjoys a woman for a while and then casts her aside when he's bored.

He pulls back and gazes into my eyes. "Let me take you on a *proper* date tonight," he says.

I raise an eyebrow. "A date? Isn't that against company policy?"

He shrugs. "I don't care anymore. I *want* you, Tessa."

My heart swells a little at hearing him say that. He wants me. What does that mean? I can't understand why he would want someone like me, but I'm not about to question him. I want him too.

When I saw that blonde Barbie doll's lips on his, it hurt even more than finding Ted fucking Kirsten. I've fallen *hard* for Bryson—for my boss.

"Okay, we can go on a date tonight," I say.

His smile widens, and he pulls me into a tight hug. What the hell am I doing?

Deep down, I have a feeling this is all going to end in heartache.

20

BRYSON

*M*y heart beats out of my chest as I watch Tessa type at her makeshift desk in the corner of my office. I'm not sure why Charlotte came on to me, but it almost ruined everything. I dismissed her instantly for unprofessional conduct.

I told Tessa the truth. Ever since I met her, I've wanted her forever. Never have I been so desperate for a woman the way I am for Tessa.

She agreed to go on a proper date with me. I feel giddy, like a little kid with a crush. I don't do feelings, but Tessa is the exception to every rule. I care about her. She's mine.

I search through some resumes that have been sent through by Human Resources. After dismissing Charlotte, I need a new secretary. Anna was always a great secretary.

According to HR, she's not qualified enough for the

position of secretary to the CEO, which is ridiculous. I fire back an email telling her I want Anna and that as the CEO, I can damn well choose.

I glance at Tessa, who is deep in a file. Her forehead crinkles as she chews on the end of her pen. We're both at a dead end of getting to the bottom of this embezzlement scheme. We're more than four weeks in and we're no closer to finding the people or person responsible. Whoever is behind it knows what they're doing. I may have to bite the bullet and call the feds in on my company.

My cock thickens in my pants as memories of the night before flood my mind. I glance up, meeting her gaze. She bites her lip, blushing. Her eyes move back to her desk. I get the feeling she's thinking about last night, too.

I stand and walk toward the windows of my office, pulling the blinds down as a precaution. My brother's not in for the rest of the day, and he's the only other person with an office on this floor. Considering I fired my secretary, we are *alone*.

I turn to find Tessa watching me. "What are you doing?"

I don't answer her and walk straight up to her chair. My arms wrap around her waist and I hoist her onto my desk. She gasps as I shove her skirt up and rub her clit through her already soaking wet panties. "Have you been fantasizing about me instead of working, Miss Clayton?"

She shakes her head. "No, *sir*."

"Don't lie to me, Tessa. You're fucking soaked right through," I growl.

She bites her lip. "Sorry, sir, yes, I've been thinking about you fucking me with your huge cock all day." She bites her lip. "I can't help it."

I capture her lips with mine in a punishing kiss before biting her bottom lip. "You're a *very* bad girl, Miss Clayton. I need to punish you."

She moans. "Please, sir."

I turn her around and press my hard arousal into her backside, gripping her hair. "What do you want, Tessa?" I ask.

"Your cock," she rasps out.

I'm lost in this woman. My common sense left me the moment I caught her staring at me. I pull her lacy panties down around her ankles and then free my cock from my pants. I drive into her hard without warning, grabbing hold of her arms behind her back, making her gasp. I'm desperate for her. Totally and utterly driven with the need to make *love* to this woman.

Make love.

Bryson Stafford doesn't make love, but sex with Tessa is different.

Shit.

Am I falling for her?

I don't care. I fuck her hard and fast—the way she likes it. The way she begged for it last night. She loves being dominated, and that makes me *want* her more, as I enjoy being in control during sex.

I slap her ass, leaving a pink mark on her creamy skin, making her moan louder. She doesn't give a shit about keeping it down, even though we are in the office in the middle of the day.

She's as lost to this as me. Her hips roll back, meeting my thrusts as I drive as deep as I can go. I'm pounding into her with no more thought or reason. My cock is ruling my brain as I dig my fingertips into her hips and hold her still, forcing her to submit to me.

The slap of flesh against flesh fills the air as I fuck her. My balls are slapping against her clit, making her cry out. Tessa doesn't care that we're in the office in the middle of the day. We're both lost to our desire for each other.

Her muscles tighten around me, squeezing my cock hard as if trying to pull me deeper. I can tell she's on the edge and I want her to come on my cock.

"That's it, Tessa, come for me, let me feel you come on my cock," I growl.

She moans, clawing at her desk beneath her. Her whole body shakes as her orgasm rips through her, making her scream, "Bryson."

I snake my arm around her waist and lift her to her feet. "Lie down."

She shifts, shaking as she lies down on her back. I remain standing in front of her, wrapping my hands around her legs and spreading them wide apart, taking in the sight of her spread for me. It's fucking beautiful. I drive my dick into her tight pussy, keeping her legs spread.

She moans as I go deep, hitting the spot that makes her scream over and over *again*. I love watching her tits bounce as we fuck, her nipples pebbled and hard, pointing right at me.

Her cheeks are bright pink, and her lips are swollen and full. I've never wanted a woman as much as I *want*, Tessa. Something tells me I'm never going to get enough of her.

I can feel the muscles in her tight pussy flutter, and I know she's close again. I drive into her even harder and faster, driving her right over the edge. She's screaming my name at the top of her lungs, and I fucking *love* it.

"Come for me, baby," I growl, as I know I'm about to *come* undone myself.

"Fuck." Tessa's head lulls back as she comes again.

Her tight muscles pull my cock further inside of her, clamping down on me and forcing me to let go, shooting my thick seed inside of her, filling her up. I'm fucking in love with this woman.

Shit.

It's true. I've fallen in *love* with my employee.

* * *

The clicking of the door opening draws my attention.

Fuck.

Who the hell is that? If they had walked in ten minutes earlier, they would have found me balls deep in my employee.

Tessa looks as mortified as I feel.

I glance over, and my heart skips a beat. A man of

average height stands in the doorway in a cheap suit, but the reason I'm so freaked out is the badge hanging on the front of his suit—a Wynton PD badge. I'd recognize it anywhere.

"Mr. Stafford?" he asks.

I stand to my feet and approach him. "Yes, Bryson Stafford, what is this about, officer?"

The man turns back to the door and motions for more officers to come in. "I'm Detective Braxton, of the Wynton PD Fraud division, working in tandem with the Internal Revenue Service and the SEC. We received some crucial information that says your company has been embezzling funds from the payroll of its employees for quite some time now. How do you answer these charges?"

I raise an eyebrow. "Are you suggesting I've got something to do with the embezzlement? If so, you are, you're mistaken." I glance at Tessa, who steps forward. "Miss Clayton brought my attention to the issue three weeks ago." I point at Tessa, whose mouth is ajar. "We've been investigating who is involved ever since. We didn't want to bring the authorities in until we were certain of who orchestrated the scheme."

The detective's brow furrows, and he shakes his head. "That seems like a rather odd thing for you to say."

Tessa steps forward. "Why would you say that?"

He looks Tessa up and down in a way that makes me want to *punch* him in the face. "Miss Clayton, is it? May I ask what your involvement is in this?"

She nods. "Well, a little over four weeks ago, I stumbled upon an expenses sheet related to the embezzlement. Someone sent it to me when it was meant for the third floor." She shuffles. "I realized something was wrong and tried to take it to my department manager, who told me I'd be fired if I didn't leave it alone." She glances at me, and I give her a reassuring smile. "I brought it to Bryson, and since then, we've been investigating it together. We have a lot of information, but we've been struggling to find who is running the scheme. Whoever it is has covered their tracks."

The detective steps closer to Tessa than I'd like. I can feel jealousy rising inside of me the way he looks at her. "Oh, you have, have you?"

"Yes, and I'm more than happy to supply you with all the information we've accrued over the last few weeks," she says.

"Yes, we'll need all the information you've found. I'm going to need you to come down to the station as well and make a statement, though."

"Yes, whatever you need," she replies.

I step forward. "Yes, we will cooperate."

The detective laughs and shakes his head. "That is almost as funny as the idea that you were investigating this problem yourself."

"Sorry?" I ask, confused by what he finds so funny.

"Considering that you're the one who is conducting the scheme. It's funny you would cooperate or run an investigation into your own embezzlement scheme."

My heart sinks into my stomach, and my mouth goes dry. I've got no idea what he is saying. "I don't know what you are talking about, detective," I say, glancing at Tessa, who looks as confused as I feel.

The detective crosses his arms over his chest. "You know nothing about your own safe deposit box at Wells Fargo Bank, with a half a million dollars in deposits over the last four weeks? You don't know anything about these payrolls health and wellness deposit receipts with your signature on them for deviation of funds?" The detective pulls out a folder from under his arm and opens it, handing it to me.

I glance down at it in shock, looking over the receipts and deposits. They all started four weeks ago. My head spins. Someone has set me up for the fall, knowing we were investigating it. I shake my head. "I've never seen these slips in my life. I've got an account at the bank, but I didn't deposit this money into it…"

Tessa grabs the file from me and scans the information. I can see her mind ticking away. She's *never* going to believe me that I'm telling the truth. She's going to think I kept her busy working by my side to keep the blame off me.

Fuck.

The blood drains from her face as she reads more. I can't lose her because of this. I don't even care about this damn company right now. All I care about is Tessa.

21

TESSA

My heart feels like it's being ripped from my chest as I read over the file. No wonder I've been having so much trouble finding who is behind this scheme.

Bryson has been blinding me from finding the truth from day one, keeping me busy chasing my tail. Not to mention fucking me. Rage bubbles up inside of me as I go over the evidence again and again.

The detective grabs the file from me. "As you can see, Bryson Stafford is behind this scheme, miss." I glance up at him. "He seems to have been distracting you from ensuring you don't stumble on the truth."

I glance at Bryson, whose face is as white as a sheet. He shakes his head. "I swear it wasn't me. Someone has set me up here," he says, his voice quieter than I've ever heard it. Bryson notices my expression and grabs my hands in his. "Tessa. It isn't true. Someone has set me *up*."

First, I walk in on the secretary kissing him and now *this*. I should have known he was just like any other man—a liar and a cheat. I can't believe I let him fool me. He has been *using* me this entire time, making me *fall* for him, all to keep the heat off of him.

He can't expect me to believe a word he says. Every single piece of evidence is against him. I'd be a *fool* to deny the truth when it's been set out so plainly in front of me. Numbers and facts never lie, but people do. It's something that I'd always believed, and as I stood staring at the man who had made me fall, it reaffirmed it again.

"You can tell it to a judge." The detective unclips the handcuffs from his belt and slaps them on Bryson's wrists.

I pull my hands from his and take a step back.

Bryson's eyes glaze with tears as he stares at me, pleading. "Tessa, you have to believe *me*."

I shake my head, unable to speak.

"Mr. Stafford, I'm placing you under arrest for embezzlement." He states, reading his right before closing the cuffs around his wrists.

Bryson's eyes remain fixed on me. "Tessa, *please*."

I hold a hand up to stop him. "Bryson, there's nothing you can say. All the evidence proves you're guilty." I turn toward the door to hide the tears prickling my eyes. He has hurt me *more* than I want him to know.

"Tessa, please, please investigate this. I promise I've been set up." His voice is desperate and sincere.

My heart skips a beat at his insinuation. Who could have set him up for this? I don't reply to his comment. The pain of betrayal right now is *too* much to overcome. I can't process his claim. I storm out of the office, too confused.

Detective Braxton calls after me, "Miss Clayton, we need you to make a statement. I'll be in *touch*."

I don't stop walking. I can't. The tears stream down my cheeks as I enter the empty elevator and press the button to the ground floor. My mind runs over everything that just happened again and again.

Could Bryson be telling the truth? I want him to be innocent more than anything. Perhaps that's why I'm entertaining the idea.

The elevator moves toward the ground floor. I'm not sure my heart could take it if I investigated this to find it was another lie.

Finally, the elevator *jerks* to a stop and opens into the lobby. I storm out of the building, not even caring what time it is. It's only two o'clock in the afternoon, but I need to getaway. I can't spend another second in The Stafford Financial Group building.

I sit on the couch in the apartment with Elena by my side. It's her night off. We sip wine together as we watch a twilight zone marathon on TLC. I need time to recover from the *biggest* shock I've had in a while.

It feels like every time I give my heart away. It's broken. The first time I'd opened myself up to a man since Ted and Bryson stamped on my heart.

Bryson isn't the man that I thought. The attempt to keep my mind off him with TV isn't working. He's a criminal and a liar. The one thing I can't shake is his claim that someone set him up. His words keep repeating in my mind.

I know it may be desperate, but deep down, I want to believe it. I want to believe that Bryson is innocent. I hold out my empty glass to Elena, who tops me up with more wine. I sit in silence, mulling over the events of the day in my mind. Elena couldn't believe it when I told her.

I left out the fact I'd slept with Bryson on four different occasions. I'd been too ashamed to tell her what happened the night I'd met him in the bar. Then when we slept together the next night, I couldn't bring myself to tell her that either. The longer it went on, the more I felt I couldn't tell her.

I'm glad I'd kept the details to myself, as it would have made explaining this to her much more difficult.

How could I have been so stupid to let my guard down again?

"Oh, I love this *one*," Elena says, as another episode starts.

"What's this one about?" I take another sip of wine.

"This is the one where her twin steals a lady's identity, and by the end, you don't know if it's the original woman or her evil twin that has taken over her life," she explains.

"Oh, that sounds scary." I snuggle deeper into the cushions and under the blanket.

"Yeah, you know we had a girl that used to work at the bar who had her identity stolen. She almost got arrested. The cops came to the bar and everything," Elena says.

"Really? What happened?"

"Well, they didn't take her in once we proved that she was in the hospital having a baby at the time that the other lady committed the crime."

"That is lucky," I say, reflecting on the story.

My mind works overtime. Identity theft happens all the time, so it wasn't impossible that someone had stolen Bryson's identity. It all seemed a little odd that Bryson would investigate a scheme he was running. If he was behind it, he would have accepted my resignation and allowed me to quit.

Elena continues, "Yeah, we had to prove she was there, though. They had to speak with the hospital and verify everything. They caught the woman posing as her."

Bryson pleaded with me to investigate this. Something that seemed a little strange was one date and time on the first deposit slip. As far as I could tell, this scheme had been going on for a while. The first deposit was on the 13th of May, at ten to six. The day Bryson and I went to dinner. What would it hurt digging a little deeper?

I stand up. "I'll be back in a second. I'm going to grab

my laptop." I head to my bedroom and grab my computer.

Bryson had arrived at the restaurant a few minutes after six, but the branch of Wells Fargo he deposited in was on the other side of town. It would have been impossible for him to travel across Wynton city during rush hour in fifteen minutes. Perhaps I was clutching at straws, but it felt possible that this was a case of identity fraud. How could he have made a deposit if he was with me?

I trawl through some data trying again to find more information, but it's sealed up tight. Whoever orchestrated this knows what the hell they are doing. Although Bryson is intelligent, he's not the best with numbers or computers to pull something like this off. Another reason to doubt that he is behind the scheme.

"Hey, Elena." I gaze up at my best friend, who glances at me. "I think Bryson is innocent."

Her eyes widen. "You do? Why?"

"One deposit was made at ten to six on the 13th of May. The date I met Bryson for dinner at the restaurant. He was with me at five minutes past six. The Wells Fargo branch is on the other side of town. I think someone has stolen his identity."

"Holy shit. That is crazy. Who do you think did it?" she asks.

"That's the thing. I've got no idea. Whoever did it has covered their tracks pretty well."

Her eyes widen further. "Wow, what are you going to do?"

It's a good question. I can't march into the police department and demand they had it wrong until I had concrete proof, which meant trying to find the person behind the scheme.

Although it was unlikely Bryson had made it across town in fifteen minutes, that wasn't concrete evidence. I need to find the perpetrator and evidence. That is what I intend to do first thing in the morning.

22

TESSA

My heart beats in my chest as I gaze up at the looming building in front of me. The Wells Fargo sign in *gold* is proudly displayed across the building.

I know I'm about to break the law, as I adjust the police badge I borrowed from Elena's room. She found it at the bar one night and has had it ever since. It was the only plan I could think of.

The intention is to walk into the bank and pose as a police officer to access their CCTV footage. If someone else deposited into Bryson's account, then they would be caught red-handed.

With one last adjustment to my blazer, I step through the doors and into the bank. A lady is sitting behind the reception desk in front of me. I walk up to her, trying to be confident. "Good morning."

"Good morning." She glances up at me and clocks the

badge on my lapel. "How can I help you, detective?" She smiles *widely* at me.

I clear my throat. "I'm working on a fraud case. I need to take a look at your CCTV from the thirteenth of May, please."

Her eyes widen. "Oh, I see. Please wait for a moment."

I nod in response as she dials on her phone. Before I know it, the manager of the bank is heading right over to me, and it makes my stomach churn.

I hope they don't know I'm not a cop. "Good morning, detective. I've been informed you need to check over some CCTV. If you would follow me, please."

Some tension eases from my shoulders. For a moment, I thought I was about to be called out for impersonating an officer who could get me some jail time, or at least community service.

I'm not even sure what this crime warrants. I hadn't checked it out before I came here. I can't believe I'm doing this to prove a man's innocence. Knowing my luck, I'll probably find Bryson depositing the cash on the CCTV.

The manager scans his badge and opens a back door into a room with some computer screens and one computer. I can't quite believe how he let me in here. I mean, he didn't even check my credentials. "You can search through any data you need. I hope there is *no* scandal I need to worry about, detective?"

"No, I hope not, sir. It's just a precaution we are

taking with a case we're working on at the moment. Nothing to worry about." I take a seat in front of the main computer.

He nods. "I'll leave you to it, then. Let me know when you've finished." I watch after him as he leaves the room, shutting the door behind him.

I'm not familiar with their security system, but after a few minutes, I get the hang of it. My fingers are shaking as work to find the footage from the thirteenth of May, and fast forward to the time I want.

I watch as a tall, dark-haired man enters the bank in a sharp suit. If you didn't know Bryson Stafford, you could take the man who walked in as Bryson. They are *very* similar looking. However, I know Bryson, perhaps too well. The man walking in isn't him. It's Theo Stafford. It *all* makes sense.

The competition his father set for him and Theo's desperation to become CEO. A flood of relief spreads through me. This was worth the risk. Coming here and finding out the man I've fallen for isn't a criminal.

I stick the USB drive into the computer and download the footage of Theo signing a slip and then making the deposit at the exact time Bryson was supposed to be there. That son of a bitch set up his brother to get the company. I can't believe it.

I head out of the back room and find the manager waiting for me. "Detective, is there anything to worry about?"

"It's difficult to say. I'm going to discuss it with my colleagues, but we will keep you informed," I lie.

As always, all these companies *ever* care about is their reputation. "Thank you, detective. Have a great day."

I nod and get the hell out of there. How did that even work? I clutch hold tightly to the USB, which proves Bryson is innocent. I detach the badge from my jacket and stuff it in my inside pocket before flagging a cab. A man slows and lets me in.

"The police department, please."

"Right away, miss."

I sit back in the seat. My mind is a mess as I go over what I've just seen. Bryson is telling the truth about not being involved in the embezzlement. It's a relief, but it doesn't mean he was telling the truth about wanting to be with me.

I've risked everything to come here today and prove he is innocent, and I know why. I'm in *love* with my boss. The question is, does he feel the same? I sigh. Or is this another one of his many flings? I'm sure I'll find out soon enough.

THE CAB COMES to a halt in front of the police station. I pay the man and step out, glancing up at the looming building in front of me. The USB is still in my grasp. I walk up the steps into the building and head for the front desk.

A woman glances up as I approach. "Can I help you?"

"I'm here to see detective Braxton about the Stafford Financial fraud case. I have some information for him."

"All right, give me a moment." The woman picks up the receiver of the phone on her desk. "Detective Braxton, I have someone here for you. They say they have information on your fraud case." The lady hangs up the receiver. "He'll be out here in a moment if you'll just wait right there." She points to a few seats in front of the desk, but I can't sit.

I step away and tap my foot on the floor, waiting for him to arrive. The echo of footsteps behind me draws my attention, and I find the detective coming my way. "Miss Clayton, what a pleasure to see you *again*." His gaze travels the length of my body.

I ignore it. "I've got some information for you if we can speak in private."

He nods. "Follow me." I follow him through a set of swing doors into the precinct. We head down a long hallway, passing a lock up and through a maze of desks before arriving at his office door. He opens it and gestures for me to take a seat in front of his desk. "Can I offer you anything to drink? Coffee, tea, water?" he asks.

"No, thank you, I'm fine."

He sits in front of his desk and clears his throat. "So, you have some information for me about the case?"

"Yes." I set the USB down on the desk in front of him, and he frowns at it before picking it up in his hand.

"What is this?" he asks.

"Proof that Bryson Stafford is innocent. It's footage from Wells Fargo at the time he made a deposit, but as you'll see on the footage, it's not him."

The detective raises an eyebrow. "How did you get CCTV footage from the bank?" he asks.

I shrug. "I asked nicely."

I watch as he puts on his glasses and slides the USB into the slot on his computer, pulling up the footage. His mouth falls open. "Theo Stafford," he mutters, almost to himself. He shakes his head. "I can't believe it."

"Why can't you believe it, detective?" I ask.

"Theo Stafford called us in on his brother. Why would he do this to his own flesh and blood?"

I nod my head. "I know the answer to that, too, detective."

His eyes widen. "You do?" he asks.

"Yes. Abraham Stafford is unwell and has assigned the two brothers each a three-month trial period as CEO. Once that is over, he intends to name his predecessor. Theo wanted to ensure he won by framing his brother and sending him to jail. It makes perfect sense."

The detective brushes his hand across his stubble dusted jaw. "Miss Clayton, if this is correct, then it's a case of embezzlement and identity fraud. It's serious. This indeed is condemning evidence, but it would help if we got a verbal confession." He gazes at me with uncertainty. "Would you be willing to take this evidence directly to Theo and confront him while wearing a wire?" he asks.

I don't even have to think about it. I nod my head instantly. "Of course, anything to free Bryson. I know he's innocent."

He smiles. "All he has spoken about in jail is you. No one has come to bail him out, which we found odd. His father and brother have both ignored us when we called them to inform them of his arrest."

My brow furrows. "Well, we know why Theo ignored you, but I wonder why Abraham did. Perhaps he's too ill."

"Perhaps." He claps his hands together. "Let's get you set up with a wire and then get you back over the office to get this confession out of Theo Stafford."

I nod and follow the detective back out of his office. My stomach is a mess of nerves, but I've got to do this. Bryson is innocent. He was telling the truth all along, and I'm the only one that can free him.

23

TESSA

It's late, but I'm sure Theo will still be here, basking in his victory. I have to hope so, anyway. I've got a reason to head to his office after leaving some files in there when I was working with Bryson. He moved *all* his stuff into the main office first thing that morning, according to the receptionist at the front desk.

I head into the elevator and select the top floor. My heart is beating out of my chest as the elevator rises. I intend to go up there and speak with him, maybe flirt a little, and see if he will open up to me. Little does he know that I already know the truth and that I'm wearing a wire to the Wynton PD stationed outside the building.

I march out of the elevator toward Bryson's office. I stutter at the sight of the new name tag already on the door: Theo Stafford - *CEO*.

What kind of brother would do that to his own flesh and blood? He doesn't deserve Bryson. Some people aren't lucky enough to still have their siblings in their life, and this asshole has framed his only brother for a crime he didn't commit. I swallow hard as Jack's face flashes into my mind.

I ball my fists and try not to let the rage and sadness get the better of me, before plastering on a smile and letting myself into the room. "Oh, I'm sorry, sir. I didn't think you'd still be here, and I wanted to come and collect my things." I nod my head toward the little desk with my files, and stationary still sat in the same place they were yesterday.

"Hello, Miss Clayton, no problem. Please, collect your belongings." He watches me as I move through his office. An arrogant smile curves onto his lips. He doesn't even hide the fact he's staring at my ass. A shiver passes down my spine. This guy is such a dirtbag.

I busy myself collecting my belongings in my handbag. His footsteps echo across the hardwood floor as he approaches. "I'm ever so sorry that you were caught in the middle of all of this," his voice is low. "Bryson pulled the wool over *all* our eyes."

I wonder what he intends to do. I turn around once I pick up my last pen and stare at him. "Are you saying you had no idea what he was up to?"

He smirks. "It is a little hard to believe that Bryson Stafford would be intelligent enough to pull this off on his own, isn't it?" He swaggers toward the sofa on the far wall and pats the seat next to him. "Have a chat with me, Tessa."

I move to sit next to him and drop my bag by the side of the sofa. "After everything, I'm not sure I can keep working here anymore. It's been so stressful."

Theo takes my hand in his, and despite wanting to punch the guy in the face, I let him. "I understand, Miss Clayton, but I'd *love* to have a woman like you working beside me." He winks and leans toward me. I realize if I'm going to get any information out of this guy, I've got to act as if I'm into this.

I let him capture my lips in a short kiss before breaking away. "Mr. Stafford, isn't it inappropriate for a CEO to kiss his employee?"

"Did that stop you from kissing my brother? I heard you and him getting rather *hot* and heavy in here the other night." Heat travels through me, settling on the back of my neck.

"Y-You did?"

He nods and leans down to kiss my neck.

This is bad. "Aren't you upset about what happened? That your brother pulled the wool over your eyes. I guess that's why he was always considered the most intelligent, running such a scheme for a long time without getting caught."

It seems I caught his attention with that, as he straightens in the chair. "More intelligent? Who the hell says that?"

I shrug. "I heard someone on the first floor saying he's always been the most intelligent out of the two of you. Isn't that true?"

He shakes his head. "It's always the stupid ones that get caught. Bryson has never had an affinity with numbers and science like I do."

"What do you mean, it's the stupid ones that get caught?"

"He got caught because he's stupid. I didn't because I'm intelligent."

"Are you saying you were involved?"

"I'm saying I was the mastermind behind it." He cocks his head to the side. "That's just between you and me." He moves his lips to mine again, and I let him kiss me, not wanting to blow my cover yet.

He pulls away. "Does that turn you on, baby? That I'm behind all of this. I'm left in the clear while Bryson goes to jail for a crime he didn't commit." He kisses my neck, and I let him, despite the sickness twisting my gut. He has confessed, which means the Wynton PD should be up here any minute to bail me out.

He stops kissing me and gazes into my eyes. "My father is *very* ill. He will die soon and leave me the company. I need someone like you by my side. Imagine how unstoppable we could be together." He doesn't even sound upset about his father's illness. He kisses my neck again, and I want to puke. When the hell are they going to arrive?

I stand, unable to stomach any more of his fawning over me. "Theo, this is *all* so much to take in." I rub the back of my neck, unsure of what to do.

He stands and grips my waist. "You can't walk away

from me now. I've told you the truth, and I need you to stay here at the company." There's an edge of a threat underlining his words.

Finally, the police bust in through the door. "Theo Stafford, don't move." Detective Braxton shouts, holding a gun in his direction.

His eyes widen, and then he glares at me. "Fucking bitch, you set me up," he shouts as I shift away from him and back behind the cops. My heart skips a beat as Bryson steps through the door and locks eyes with me.

"Hello, little brother," he says, grabbing my hand as he steps up next to me. I smile up at him. "I'm afraid it is over." He pulls the wire out from beneath my blouse. "We heard everything. Not to mention, Tessa has footage of you entering Wells Fargo posing as me."

He shakes his head in shock, unable to stay anything. Detective Braxton tackles Theo to the ground, and they cuff him, although he is trying to hit anyone that gets near him. He ends up kicking on the floor like a kid having a tantrum.

The police officers drag him out of the office, leaving me alone with Bryson. He looks a little torn as he watches the door where his brother is dragged out. "I can't quite believe it," he mutters, shaking his head.

I shift to stand in front of him and take his chin in my hands. "I'm so sorry, Bryson." I shake my head. "I'm sorry I ever doubted you." I gaze deep into his blue eyes.

He smiles at me. "Tessa, you have no reason to apologize. You saved me from prison and proved I'm innocent. How can I ever thank you?"

My heart breaks a little as I wonder if he feels the same way about me as I feel about him. Tears prickle my eyes, and I turn away and take a few steps away.

"What's wrong?" he asks.

I clear my throat. "Did you mean it? Before, when you said…" My throat closes up, and I can't even ask him. Tears spill from my eyes as the fear of heartbreak and rejection paralyzes me.

He places a hand on my shoulder and spins me around. "Did I mean what, Tessa?"

I shake my head and gaze at the floor. He can't see me cry. He can't see how vulnerable he makes me. "It doesn't matter." I try to walk past him, but he stops me.

He pulls me into his arms and lifts my chain to look at him. "Did I mean that I want to date you for real? Hell yeah, I meant it." He shakes his head. "Tessa, I know we haven't known each other that long, but I've fallen for you, hard." He presses his lips against my own. "When they arrested me, do you know the one thing I worried about the most?"

I shake my head in answer.

"Never seeing you again. I didn't care about the company or the money, only you."

I can't quite believe what I'm hearing. My heart beats fast as I pull him toward me and kiss him.

He pulls away and gazes into my eyes. "I love you, Tessa Clayton."

"I love you, too," I say, past the pain coating the sides of my throat.

He pulls me into him again, and we get lost in each other until someone clears their throat behind us. Detective Braxton is standing in the doorway. "Sorry to interrupt. I wanted to let you know we're finished up and heading back to the precinct now."

"Did you get enough evidence to clear, Bryson?"

He smiles widely. "Thanks to you, yes. Bryson is clear, and Theo will go to jail for what he did. There's no way he's going to weasel his way out of this one." He turns back toward the door. "Both of you take it easy." He gives us a knowing smile and leaves the two of us alone in Bryson's office.

Bryson turns to the door and locks it before giving me a look that sends a shiver of need through me. "Come here," he demands.

I walk toward him, and he pulls me against his muscular chest. "I've missed you," he whispers into my ear.

My brow furrows. "It's only been twenty-four hours."

He kisses my neck, and I moan. "Twenty-four hours too long, baby." He trails kisses up my neck. "I couldn't stop thinking about you the entire time."

"I'm so glad it wasn't true. At first, I thought—"

Bryson silences me with a kiss. "It's all over now." He trails kisses along my neck and shoulder, unbuttoning my blouse. I submit to him, allowing him to undress me. The look in his eyes is a mix of adoration and lust.

He lifts me into his arms and carries me over to the sofa I'd been sitting on with Theo. His touch is soft and slow, as he works my skirt loose and slides it down my legs. He frees himself from his clothes and stands, towering above me, naked. The sight of him makes my mouth water. He shifts to kneel between my legs and closes his mouth over the bundle of nerves at the apex of my thighs.

"Bryson," I gasp his name as he thrusts *two* fingers inside of me, curling them to hit the spot that makes my toes curl. Within seconds of his mouth working my clit, I'm ready to tip over the edge.

He stops at the moment I'm about to come undone and withdraws his fingers, making me whimper in protest. My body tenses as I feel him circle my back hole with his finger, wet with my arousal. "Relax," he says, as he slides his finger through the tight muscles of my ass.

It's so fucking dirty. My boss has his finger up my ass in his office, and I can't quite believe it. The sensation makes everything ten times more pleasurable as he thrusts his finger in and out of me. I've tried it before and enjoyed it, but never with a man endowed like Bryson.

"Do you like my finger in your asshole?" he growls.

I tremble beneath him and nod. "Yes, are you going to fuck me there?" I ask.

His eyes are dilated with pure desire. He shakes his head, and my stomach dips. I wanted him to.

"Why not?"

His eyes narrow. "Do you want me to fuck your ass?"

I glance between his thick, long length and his finger, which is thrusting in and out. Would it fit? I'm so damn needy. I don't seem to care. "Yes, I want you to fuck my ass, sir."

He growls and kisses me hard, his finger still pumping in and out of my hole, making me moan. "Not today, Tessa. You're not ready for me."

The pressure building within me is the promise of release soon as he lights up every nerve with his finger and licks my pussy at the same time. I love the way it feels. It's so filthy, but so good. He doesn't let up as I squirm beneath him. His teeth graze over my clit and pleasure explodes through me.

"Fuck, Bryson," I scream his name as I come apart with his mouth on me. He's still licking my juices from my dripping wet slit, his finger still pumping in and out of my back hole, stirring the need to feel him inside me. "I need you inside me," I rasp out.

His aquamarine eyes light up as he fists his huge length with his hand, sitting back on his haunches. I take in the sight of him. He looks amazing with his muscles straining as he runs his hand from root to tip of his huge cock between his legs. "How much do you need me?"

"I need you so bad, Bryson, please."

"I love you begging me," He growls as he shifts between my thighs and positions the head of his cock in line with my entrance, sliding it between my wet lips. He glides into me, gazing into my eyes as, inch by inch, he sinks deeper.

I link my hands behind his neck and pull his lips to mine, kissing him as he moves in and out of me, slow and deep. The pressure inside me wells again the moment he stretches my pussy, filling me. He's driving deep in the most pleasurable way, hitting that part of me that no one ever has before him. He pulls back from the kiss and licks a path down my neck as he continues to fuck me, harder and faster now. The intensity is growing as I claw my fingertips into his back, needing more of him.

He stops when I'm about to come and leans towards me, kissing my lips and then nipping at my ear. "On your hands and knees," he commands.

I turn around and shift to the floor, dropping to my knees and baring myself to him. He thrusts his cock inside me without warning, and next, I feel his slick finger back inside my tight hole.

Fuck.

His grunts become animalistic as he drives into me hard and fast, hitting the spot inside me that promises release. He fucks my pussy with his cock and my ass with his finger. I gasp as he adds another slick finger into my ass, stretching it out more. I know I won't last long, as he pounds me like this with his fingers in there. It's filthy, but it turns me on like nothing *ever* has.

"Bryson, I'm coming," I scream as the pressure wells to breaking point and a far more intense orgasm rocks through me.

His cock hardens inside me, and then he grunts against my neck as he comes undone too, shooting his seed deep inside of me. We rest together for a moment; The rasping of our heavy breathing fills the air.

He breaks the silence. "You're so fucking filthy, Tessa, begging me to fuck your ass."

I can't help but moan even though I'm spent. "I want you to."

He nips my ear with his teeth. "I will. I'm going to claim all your holes, but not today. We best get dressed," he mutters into my ear.

He retreats from on top of me and turns to find our clothes scattered about his office. I watch the man I love in awe as he heads to the bathroom to clean up. He's more perfect than I ever could have believed I deserved. When he returns, he passes me my skirt and blouse.

I pull them back on before turning to face Bryson, who is dressed before me.

"I think it's about time I take you on a proper date." He winks.

I can't help but laugh. "Yeah, well, normally, you go on a date and then have sex."

He walks up to me and wraps his arms around my waist. "I intend to make love to you after as well," he whispers in my ear.

I moan, shocked at how wanton I am for this man. I've just come twice, but it's not enough, it's never enough. Bryson is my *addiction*.

24

BRYSON

I sit in the dreary gray interrogation room across a scratched-up aluminum table from my father. We've been brought in to answer some routine questions. I'd spent some time in the past in places like this, waiting for my dad to come to bail me out. This time I'm here because my brother is a greedy idiot. My dad isn't looking too well, and I feel bad that he's been dragged into this.

"Are you okay?" I ask.

He looks up from his lap and forces a weak smile. "I'm fine. I can't believe Theo attempted to frame you." He draws in a shaky breath. "I wish I'd listened to him and handed the company over to both of you. At least he wouldn't be in prison."

I feel torn by his sentiments. On the one hand, I don't want my brother to spend time in prison, but on the other, he would have let me spend the time in prison so he could have the company. I shake my head. "Theo isn't an honest person. He wanted the company so bad that he tried to submit me to prison and derision. That is plain wrong."

He looks up and nods. "You're right, son." He runs a hand through his graying hair. "It's hard to see one of your children facing prison when you know you're not going to be around much longer. I'll be dead before Theo is released."

I nod in understanding. In the last months of my dad's life, Theo will be locked away. I'd never seen my father look so broken in all my life. He is a tired old man who has lost *all* his spirit. Theo might have just killed him off with this. I'm not sure he can get over the heartache of his son going to prison.

Detective Braxton entered the room and gave us both a weak smile. "Thank you for coming down here today, both of you." He glances at my father. "I know you're not in the best state of health at the moment, Mr. Stafford. It's appreciated."

My father nods. "Of course, anything I can do to help."

The detective takes a seat. "As you're aware, we've got all the evidence we need to charge Theo."

We nod together. "How long do you expect him to serve?"

"He will serve a minimum of a year, and there will be a fine to be paid." He turns his attention to my father. "Am I right to think you've volunteered to pay the fine?"

My father nods, to my surprise. "Why can't Theo pay it?"

"Theo has no money. He has gambled everything he ever owned away for years."

My eyes widen. "Gambled? How did I never know about this?"

My dad sighs. "He never wanted you to know. He's suffered from a gambling addiction for a long while now. I'm happy to pay the fine."

I shake my head. All this time, I believed I was the only one with problems. It turns out Theo had his own weaknesses, too.

"I have to ask both of you whether you knew of Theo's scheme. It's just routine."

"Of course, I had no idea. Theo framed me for it, so he wasn't keeping me in the loop."

Detective Braxton nods and then turns his attention to my dad. "How about you, Mr. Stafford?"

My dad shakes his head. "I had a feeling he was up to something dodgy from some things he would say in passing, but I never knew the extent of what he was up to…" My dad's eyes fill with tears, and he coughs violently.

I stand and move to the other side, placing a reassuring hand on his shoulder. "Detective, my father isn't very well at all. Is this really necessary?"

Detective Braxton gives him a weak smile. "We need to know to what extent your father was aware of the embezzlement. He was, after all, CEO while it was occurring."

My eyes widen at his insinuation. "My father had nothing to do with it. This is to do with Theo trying to frame me so he could win the company."

The detective nods. "I need to hear that from your father, Bryson."

My dad pats my hand. "Let me speak with the detective. How about you wait outside?"

What the hell is happening here? Is my father saying he had something to do with all this? Despite my curiosity to learn more, I nod and head out of the interrogation room. A young officer greets me. "If you would like to wait for your father, you can do so in the waiting area," he instructs.

I nod and follow him to the area. Tessa is waiting for me there. She agreed to come with me for moral support. "Where is your father?"

I take a seat next to her. "They need to ask him more questions…" I hesitate, unsure whether to tell her that my father may have known more about the scheme than first believed. "The detective seems to think my dad had knowledge of the scheme." The moment I say it out loud, my throat coats with pain. I hope to hell he had no idea that Theo intended to use it against me.

"I'm sorry," Tessa says, placing a hand over mine.

We sit together in comfortable silence for what feels like *forever*. Finally, Detective Braxton comes out with my father in tow. "Bryson, can you come with us for a moment?"

I glance at Tessa, and she gives me a smile. "I'll see

you in a minute." I squeeze her hand one last time.

We enter a private room, and the detective shuts the door. "Bryson, your father was aware of Theo's scheme. He brushed it under the carpet while CEO to protect him, unaware of the fact he was setting you up for the fall."

My mouth falls open, and I gaze at my father. "Why would you do that? You've always told us how important it is to make money."

My dad sighs. "I know, son. Theo is my child. There was no way I was going to hand him into the police, but obviously, I would have done things differently if I knew his true intention."

"Did you even try to confront him about it?"

My dad shakes his head. "I didn't want him panicking and doing something stupid, so I turned a blind eye."

"What does this mean?"

Detective Braxton clears his throat. "It means your father could be tried as an accomplice to your brother's scheme. Given his physical state, we won't be pursuing that."

My dad's eyes widen. "Is there no way that I could take the fall for this and save Theo from prison?"

The detective shakes his head. "Sir, your son will answer for his crimes. There's nothing you can do to change that."

My dad sighs, tears flooding his eyes. "I see."

"All of my questions have been answered. You're both free to leave. I will be in touch if necessary."

I move to help my dad stand, and we head back out to meet Tessa. My dad gives her a thoughtful look. "Who is this?"

"Tessa, she's the accounting analyst who helped me investigate the scheme." I pause a moment, wondering if he will scorn me for my next confession. "We're also dating."

My dad looks startled. "Son, you do realize that's against company policy, considering you're the CEO."

"It's not a fling, so I don't see what the problem is. Tessa and I are in a committed relationship."

My dad rubs his chin. "I've got to admit. I never thought I'd see my son commit to someone. I'm happy that you've proven me wrong." The smile on his face reaches his eyes for once. "How about we all head over to my place and I order in some food?" he asks, glancing at Tessa. "I'd like to get to know the woman who put a stop to my son's philandering while I still have the chance."

"I'd like that," Tessa says, gazing at me for an answer.

"Let's do it." I take hold of my father's arm and help him out onto the street. Tom is waiting outside. "Hey, Tom, we're all going to head over to my father's if that's okay?"

"Of course, sir." Tom scurries to help my father into the car. Tessa follows, and then I settle in beside her. She takes my hand and squeezes it.

As I glance over at the woman next to me, I can't believe how lucky I am to have her by my side.

* * *

Later that evening, we're all getting on better than I could have hoped for. For the first time in a long while, I've seen my father smile. Tessa makes a joke, and my dad laughs.

"I like this one, Bryson. You better keep hold of her. She reminds me of your mother."

My heart swells, and pain coats my throat, hearing my father speak about my mother. She always was a very intelligent and independent woman. She died when I was six years old, and sometimes I struggle to remember her.

Tessa excuses herself to go to the bathroom, leaving me alone with my father. "Bryson, I want you to know that I'm proud of the man you've become."

I can feel the lump returning to my throat, hearing my father say those words. The words I've *longed* to hear him say.

"I've always been proud of you, no matter what, because you're my son. Now, seeing you happy with a woman who is *too* good for you makes me even more proud. I meant what I said. Don't let her go."

I sigh. "I won't, Dad, she's amazing."

"It makes me sad that Theo isn't in as good a place as you are right now. I know that he will find his way even if I'm not here to see it. At least I know the company is in good hands."

I smile, a sense of pride and happiness flooding me. I never thought my dad would say that to me. He believes I'm good enough to run the company. It means the world to me.

"I'm sorry I haven't been around much. I hope to make up for that now."

Tears cloud my father's eyes, and I stand up and move to give him a hug. Tessa returns and looks unsure about entering, but I beckon her in. She walks toward me, and I wrap my arm around her. "How are you feeling, Dad? Would you like us to leave you to get some rest?"

He shakes his head. "I think I'll retire now, but I asked Tom to head home. Avery has set up a room for you and Tessa to stay the night. I thought it might be nice for us to have breakfast together in the morning and then maybe go for a walk in the park?" He looks so hopeful that there's no way I can say no.

"Sure, if it's okay with Tessa." I glance at her, and she is beaming at me.

"That sounds wonderful, thank you, Mr. Stafford."

"Perfect. I'll see you both in the morning. Avery will show you to your room." He nods toward a woman standing in the corner. "And, Tessa, please call me Abraham."

She nods. "Good night," Tessa and I say in unison, as we watch my father make his way toward the door where his caregiver is waiting for him.

He may not have long left, but I intend to make the most of the lost time. Tessa pulls me into a hug as we stand there together in silence for a while.

She makes me believe I can tackle anything. Perhaps, with her by my side, I can.

EPILOGUE

TESSA

I run a hand through my long, thick hair and sigh as I scan the deal in front of me. Although it's almost five o'clock, I'm still going over some important last-minute details of a deal I've been working on for the past three months.

This client is one of the hardest I've dealt with. I thought everything was fine until he sent back some revisions. I need to get it finalized today, and the time is ticking away. If I don't get it done before the end of the day, the client might go elsewhere.

The click of the door opening draws my attention. Bryson stands in the doorway, smiling at me. It's been tough on him since his father died three months ago, so I've been taking more of a lead here at the firm.

"Hey, beautiful," he says, shutting the door behind him.

"Hey, what's up?" I ask.

He shrugs. "I want to take you somewhere."

I frown at him. "I've got to complete this deal for the Braithwaite account tonight."

He shakes his head. "I've asked Roger to deal with it. It will be in capable hands. We're going on vacation right now."

"Bryson, we can't up and leave with no warning. I've not even packed."

He walks toward me with a mischievous grin on his face. "I've already packed for you. We're going now, and there is no discussion. You've been working far *too* hard." He lifts my hand to his lips and kisses the back of it.

I sigh. "Okay, let me get my—"

He presses his lips to mine, silencing me. I moan against him. It is crazy how even after a year together, we can't seem to get enough of each other. In fact, my need for him only grows the more I get to know him.

"No need to get anything. Come on." He pulls me from my seat, and I grab my handbag on the way out. He gets in the elevator and presses the top floor. I frown at him. "Why are we going to the roof?"

He smiles. "It's the fastest means of transport."

My heart rate accelerates. I hope he doesn't intend to put me in a helicopter. That is not my idea of a good time. Those things are death traps. He pulls me back against him and rubs my shoulders. "Relax, I'll protect you," he whispers into my ear.

"Bryson, you know I hate helicopters. They're dangerous."

He shakes his head. "We won't be in it for too long. Relax, baby."

The elevator opens to allow us onto the roof, and the sight of the helicopter only increases my anxiety. He grabs hold of my hand and leads me toward it. "Don't worry. Everything will be all right." I gaze up into his eyes, knowing I can trust him. I never thought I'd trust a man again after Ted, but I trust Bryson with my life.

We sit in the helicopter, and Bryson straps me in. "Are you going to tell me where we're going?"

He shakes his head. "No, it's a surprise."

My heart beats as the propellers whiz above us. The drone of the helicopter makes the anxiety worse and even more so when we lift into the air. My nails dig into the armrest as I cling on. Bryson's arm snakes around my back, pulling me into him. The protective move is sweet, but it doesn't help the sickness twisting my gut. It feels like we're in the air forever. Bryson keeps gazing out the window, but I daren't look.

Finally, we touch down, and I let out a long exhale. Bryson helps me down from the helicopter, and I gaze around to find we've landed in a field in the middle of nowhere. "Where are we?"

"I told you it's a surprise. You'll find out soon enough." He kisses me before stepping out of the helicopter.

The pilot grabs two hiking bags out of the luggage hold and hands us each one. "Is that all you need, sir?"

Bryson nods. "Yes, thanks, Arthur. You can return to the city."

"Are we going hiking?"

He smiles at me. "Sort of. You said I need to go on a vacation to the countryside. That's what we're doing."

I throw the hiking bag over my shoulder and follow Bryson toward a forest. We walk for what feels like forever in comfortable silence. A small cabin comes into view, with a lake in front of it.

My heart skips a beat as I recognize it. My family used to come here for vacation *all* the time. Tears trickle down my cheek as I remember the last time we came here. It was the summer before Jack's death.

"How did you know about this place?"

Bryson glances at me. "Your mom told me about it. She said you used to love it out here, so I thought…"

I nod and step closer to the lake we used to swim in as children. "I haven't been here since…"

"Since your brother died?"

I nod, and more tears flood my eyes. He moves to pull me into a hug. "I'm sorry. I didn't want to upset you."

I shake my head. "No, it is perfect. I want to enjoy this place again with you." I smile at him.

"Good," he says, dragging me toward the cabin. "Because I bought the place."

My eyes widen as he grabs a key out of his pocket and waves it in the air. "You did what?"

"I bought it for you and me to enjoy. A place we can escape to whenever we want to be alone, together."

He kisses me hard before pulling back and winking at me. "Not to mention, no one can hear your screams here while I fuck you, and we can be as loud as we want."

I chuckle at that. We've had some noise complaints in our apartment building. I can get *too* loud. It was embarrassing when we had the call from management, but Bryson argued that it was our damn apartment, and he could fuck me as hard as he wants. Afterward, once he calmed down, he agreed to keep the sound to a minimum.

He opens the door, and it's as I remember it. "We can do it up how we want, or keep it as it is."

I smile at him. "I like it how it is, but I wouldn't mind adding a few touches to it."

He kisses me. "Get ready for dinner. I've got something set up for you by the lake."

I cock my head and give him an uncertain glance. "What are you up to?"

He shakes his head. "Nothing, put on the sexy dress I packed for you. I'll see you down by the lake." He turns away and leaves me staring after him.

I get dressed, looking around the cabin as I do. It's bittersweet as I gaze around the cabin. I spent so many happy summers with my brother and parents. My hand settles on my belly, knowing that I need to tell Bryson tonight.

Perhaps we can make some new happy memories here as a family. I've known I'm a few weeks pregnant since last Thursday. It was a shock, considering I'm on the pill, but it seems it's not one-hundred percent safe.

I step into the main bedroom and set my pack down on the floor. The dress Bryson has packed more like an undergarment. I can tell he intends to make sure we make the most of being so isolated.

It is so short you can almost see my ass. The cleavage is more revealing than I'd ever show in public. I might as well go out there wearing my underwear, but it makes me smile. He'd never let me wear this in front of anyone else. He is far too possessive, and I love that about him. He *owns* me. I wouldn't have it any other way.

I step out of the cabin and head down the overgrown path toward the lake. My heart skips a beat as I notice a candlelit table and light music playing. It looks stunning. Bryson is wearing a tight shirt and pants.

"What's all this about?" I ask.

He turns and smiles at me. "Goddamn, you look sexy in that dress." He pulls me into him and kisses my neck, making me moan. I'm not going to be able to focus on dinner if he keeps doing that to me. I notice the metal platters resting on a table. "Did you order in?"

He nods. "Kind of. Avery came over earlier and got everything prepared for us."

I twirl around, taking in the lake lit by fairy lights strung around trees. It looks more magical than it *ever* has before. I turn back to Bryson to find him down on one knee. He smiles up at me as my brow furrows.

"Tessa, ever since I met you, I knew I couldn't live my

life without you by my side. Will you marry me?" he asks, holding out a box housing a large engagement ring.

I glance down at him, unable to see through the tears clouding my eyes. "Yes, of course, I'll marry you." I'm breathless and happier than I've ever been in my entire life. This is how it should feel when someone asks you to marry you.

Bryson slips the ring onto my finger and then stands to kiss me. "I love you, Bryson."

"I love you too, baby." He gropes my ass. "And I love the way your ass looks in this dress."

My smile falters as my hand lands on my belly. "I have some news of my own…" Although he just proposed to me, anxiety floods me. We've never spoken about whether he wants kids. I'm scared about how he might react.

"What is it? Are you okay?"

I smile. "Yes, I hope so…" I grab his hand in mine. "I went to the doctor last week and was trying to find the right time to tell you, but I'm pregnant."

Bryson blinks twice. "Pregnant?"

I nod. "Y-Yes, I know we haven't discussed having children and—"

Bryson pulls me to him and kisses me. "It's amazing news. It's a bit ahead of schedule, but we can deal with it."

"So, you're happy?"

"Happy is an understatement. I'm ecstatic. I can't wait to start a family with you, Tessa."

Tears of joy well in my eyes. "I wasn't sure what you'd say." The tears spill from my eyes down my cheek.

He wipes them from my face and presses his lips against mine. "I say that I'm the luckiest man in the world to have found you."

"Wait until I tell Elena she's going to be the maid of honor and a godparent. She's going to go mental," I say, laughing.

"I'll ensure I'm far away from that one. I love Elena, but she is the *most* dramatic woman I've ever met."

I laugh at that.

He glances at the silver platters on the side. "I'm hungry for your ass rather than food," he growls, grabbing hold of my hips and pulling me toward him.

His length is as hard as stone as he presses it into me. "Then fuck my ass," I moan, wanting to feel my fiancé's cock stretching me out.

He groans. "I need to get the lube." He steps away, but I grab hold of his wrist and pull him back, forcing his hand under my dress and guiding his finger to my already lubed hole.

He groans. "Fuck, you're perfect. Did I tell you that?"

I smirk at him and force him down onto the grass by the lake, kissing him with all the love and passion I feel for him, pouring it into the kiss.

My hands move to pull his t-shirt over his head and then work on removing his belt. His rough, large hands snake under my dress, pulling it off me and exposing my already pebbled nipples, which he pulls into his mouth one by one, making my back arch.

"Bryson..." He kisses my breasts and trails his lips along my collarbone and then my neck.

I free his belt, removing his pants and pawing his hard length through his boxers. He grunts against me as I free him and stroke his thick, hot length from root to tip.

"I want you right now," he groans, grabbing my hips and forcing me to straddle his cock.

My pussy is soaking wet. I lower myself down over his hard cock as he captures my lips. He bites my lip as I ride him, rising and falling harder and faster on his length.

He kisses my neck and collarbone before nipping my ear. "You feel so fucking good," he groans as he pinches my nipples between his finger and thumb.

I'm about to come already. My muscles are unfolding around his hard length. "Shit, I'm coming," I say, speeding up as I drive myself over the edge. I keep riding him though, chasing more pleasure as his huge cock builds it almost instantly.

"I'm ready to fuck your ass, baby," he groans. "Get on your knees, now," he commands.

I love the way he dominates and commands me. I get off his lap and bend over, baring myself to him, my ass high in the air, ready and lubed for his thick length. He rubs the head of his cock against the tight ring of muscles and teases me, making me beg him. "Please, Bryson, fuck my ass."

"Hmm, you know I love it when you beg me, baby."

He slaps my ass, and I buck my hips, trying to sink his cock into me. He grips hips, holding me still. "I'm in control," he growls.

"Fuck, Bryson. I need you inside me *now*."

He presses against my hole, and it relaxes, sinking him in inch by inch until his balls are resting against my drenched pussy. I can barely think straight at how good it feels. White creeps into my vision as the pleasure threatens to make me come before he even moves inside me.

The noise he makes is animalistic as he moves in and out. He grabs hold of my throat and pulls me up toward him, fucking me still. "I'll never tire of fucking your perfect little asshole," he mutters into my ear.

I moan as he fucks me harder and harder, holding me by the throat and kissing my neck and the spot below my ear that sends shivers down my spine. It's so filthy, but I love it.

Bryson's arms snake around my waist, shifting me onto my side, while his cock is still buried inside me, and resting his lips against the back of my neck. His finger finds the sensitive bundle of nerves at the apex of my thighs, and he rubs my swollen clit, lighting up every pleasure center inside me. It amplifies the amazing sensation of his cock stretching me.

He fucks me hard until I can't take it anymore, and every muscle in my body unfolds as I tip over the edge of oblivion. My body clamps down around his dick, milking his seed as his cock fills my ass up with his cum, shooting rope after rope inside me. Our heavy breathing fills the air, as we rest on the grass together, totally spent.

He holds me tight in his arms, kissing my neck and shoulder. "I love you, baby," he says, nipping my ear.

"I love you too," I reply, feeling happier than I've ever felt in my life.

Thank you for reading Filthy Boss, I hope you enjoyed Tessa's and Bryson's story.

If you'd like to read more, the next book in the Forbidden series is Filthy Professor. Available on KU and to buy at Amazon.

I know the number one rule as a professor — never under any circumstances get involved with a student.

I'd never had a problem sticking to the rules, until the fated first day of the semester when Sasha Harman walks into the lecture hall of my British Literature class.

She captures my attention like no other woman ever has. She is beautiful and intelligent.

I try to fight it, perhaps not hard enough, but I try. But, once I taste of her, I know I can't stop.

Then she tells me she's a virgin and I know there is no way in hell I'm letting her go. I'm going to claim my student and make her mine, and nothing can stop me.

Filthy Professor is a steamy and hot forbidden romance between professor and student with an over the top possessive alpha male. It has hot scenes and bad language.

Filthy Professor is a safe story in the Wynton series with no cliffhanger, no cheating, and a guaranteed HEA.

ALSO BY BIANCA COLE

The Syndicate Academy

Corrupt Educator: A Dark Forbidden Mafia Academy Romance

Cruel Bully: A Dark Mafia Academy Romance

Chicago Mafia Dons

Merciless Defender: A Dark Forbidden Mafia Romance

Violent Leader: A Dark Enemies to Lovers Captive Mafia Romance

Evil Prince: A Dark Arranged Marriage Romance

Boston Mafia Dons Series

Cruel Daddy: A Dark Mafia Arranged Marriage Romance

Savage Daddy: A Dark Captive Mafia Roamnce

Ruthless Daddy: A Dark Forbidden Mafia Romance

Vicious Daddy: A Dark Brother's Best Friend Mafia Romance

Wicked Daddy: A Dark Captive Mafia Romance

New York Mafia Doms Series

Her Irish Daddy: A Dark Mafia Romance

Her Russian Daddy: A Dark Mafia Romance

Her Italian Daddy: A Dark Mafia Romance

Her Cartel Daddy: A Dark Mafia Romance

Romano Mafia Brother's Series

Her Mafia Daddy: A Dark Daddy Romance

Her Mafia Boss: A Dark Romance

Her Mafia King: A Dark Romance

Bratva Brotherhood Series

Bought by the Bratva: A Dark Mafia Romance

Captured by the Bratva: A Dark Mafia Romance

Claimed by the Bratva: A Dark Mafia Romance

Bound by the Bratva: A Dark Mafia Romance

Taken by the Bratva: A Dark Mafia Romance

Wynton Series

Filthy Boss: A Forbidden Office Romance

Filthy Professor: A First Time Professor And Student Romance

Filthy Lawyer: A Forbidden Hate to Love Romance

Filthy Doctor: A Fordbidden Romance

Royally Mated Series

Her Faerie King: A Faerie Royalty Paranormal Romance

Her Alpha King: A Royal Wolf Shifter Paranormal Romance

Her Dragon King: A Dragon Shifter Paranormal Romance

Her Vampire King: A Dark Vampire Romance

ABOUT THE AUTHOR

I love to write stories about over the top alpha bad boys who have heart beneath it all, fiery heroines, and happily-ever-after endings with heart and heat. My stories have twists and turns that will keep you flipping the pages and heat to set your kindle on fire.

For as long as I can remember, I've been a sucker for a good romance story. I've always loved to read. Suddenly, I realized why not combine my love of two things, books and romance?

My love of writing has grown over the past four years and I now publish on Amazon exclusively, weaving stories about dirty mafia bad boys and the women they fall head over heels in love with.

If you enjoyed this book please follow her on Amazon, Bookbub or any of the below social media platforms for alerts when more books are released.

Printed in Great Britain
by Amazon